J GN DISNEY
Maine, Regis
Cinderella : the story of
the movie in comics

042220

Disney

# Cinderella

## THE STORY OF THE MOVIE IN COMICS

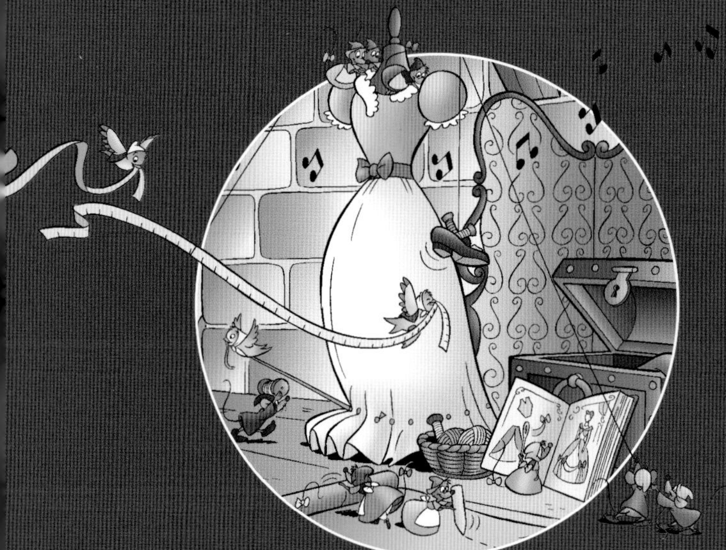



DARK HORSE BOOKS

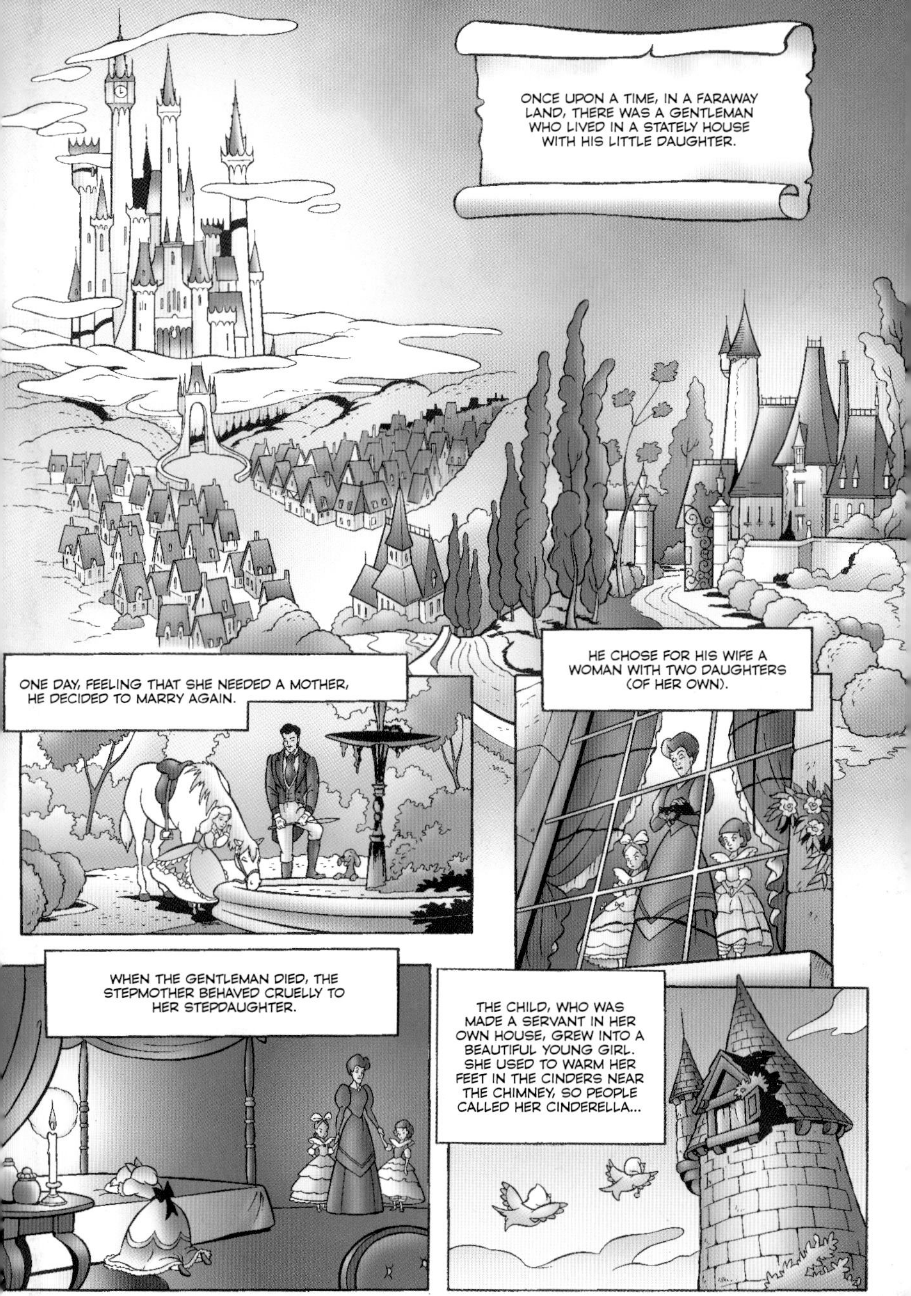
ONCE UPON A TIME, IN A FARAWAY LAND, THERE WAS A GENTLEMAN WHO LIVED IN A STATELY HOUSE WITH HIS LITTLE DAUGHTER.
ONE DAY, FEELING THAT SHE NEEDED A MOTHER, HE DECIDED TO MARRY AGAIN.
HE CHOSE FOR HIS WIFE A WOMAN WITH TWO DAUGHTERS (OF HER OWN).
WHEN THE GENTLEMAN DIED, THE STEPMOTHER BEHAVED CRUELLY TO HER STEPDAUGHTER.
THE CHILD, WHO WAS MADE A SERVANT IN HER OWN HOUSE, GREW INTO A BEAUTIFUL YOUNG GIRL. SHE USED TO WARM HER FEET IN THE CINDERS NEAR THE CHIMNEY, SO PEOPLE CALLED HER CINDERELLA...

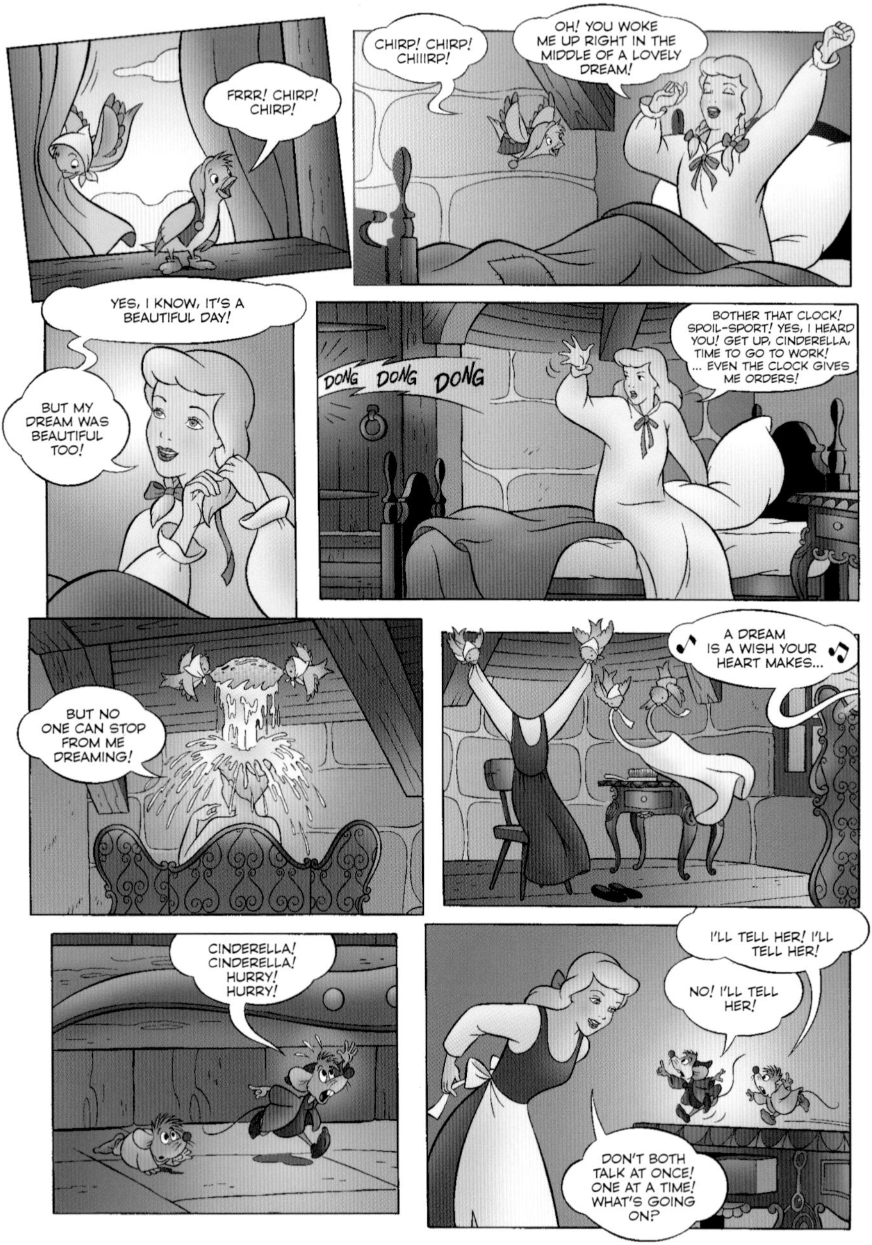
FRRR! CHIRP! CHIRP!
CHIRP! CHIRP! CHIIIRP!
OH! YOU WOKE ME UP RIGHT IN THE MIDDLE OF A LOVELY DREAM!
YES, I KNOW, IT'S A BEAUTIFUL DAY!
BUT MY DREAM WAS BEAUTIFUL TOO!
DONG DONG DONG
BOTHER THAT CLOCK! SPOIL-SPORT! YES, I HEARD YOU! GET UP, CINDERELLA, TIME TO GO TO WORK! ... EVEN THE CLOCK GIVES ME ORDERS!
BUT NO ONE CAN STOP FROM ME DREAMING!
A DREAM IS A WISH YOUR HEART MAKES...
CINDERELLA! CINDERELLA! HURRY! HURRY!
I'LL TELL HER! I'LL TELL HER!
NO! I'LL TELL HER!
DON'T BOTH TALK AT ONCE! ONE AT A TIME! WHAT'S GOING ON?

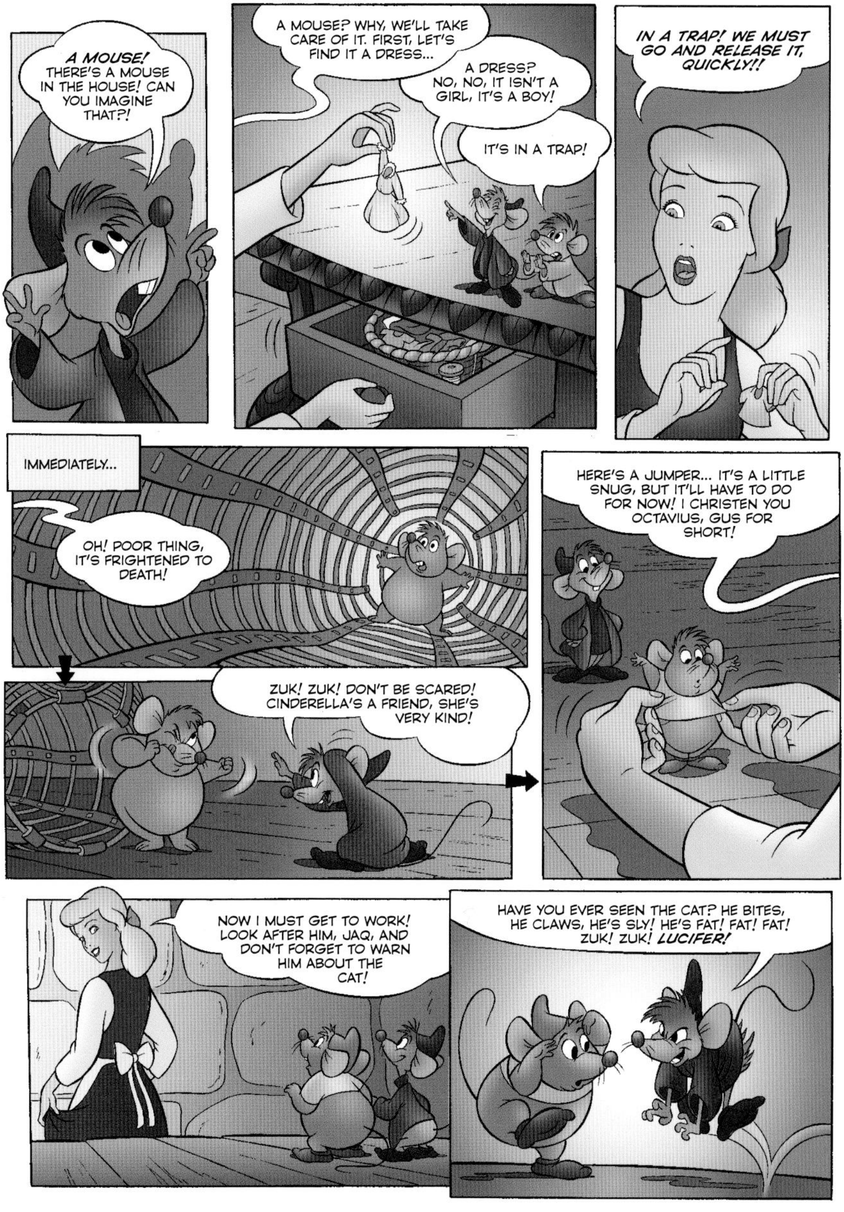
A MOUSE! THERE'S A MOUSE IN THE HOUSE! CAN YOU IMAGINE THAT?!
A MOUSE? WHY, WE'LL TAKE CARE OF IT. FIRST, LET'S FIND IT A DRESS...
A DRESS? NO, NO, IT ISN'T A GIRL, IT'S A BOY!
IT'S IN A TRAP!
IN A TRAP! WE MUST GO AND RELEASE IT, QUICKLY!!
IMMEDIATELY...
OH! POOR THING, IT'S FRIGHTENED TO DEATH!
ZUK! ZUK! DON'T BE SCARED! CINDERELLA'S A FRIEND, SHE'S VERY KIND!
HERE'S A JUMPER... IT'S A LITTLE SNUG, BUT IT'LL HAVE TO DO FOR NOW! I CHRISTEN YOU OCTAVIUS, GUS FOR SHORT!
NOW I MUST GET TO WORK! LOOK AFTER HIM, JAQ, AND DON'T FORGET TO WARN HIM ABOUT THE CAT!
HAVE YOU EVER SEEN THE CAT? HE BITES, HE CLAWS, HE'S SLY! HE'S FAT! FAT! FAT! ZUK! ZUK! LUCIFER!

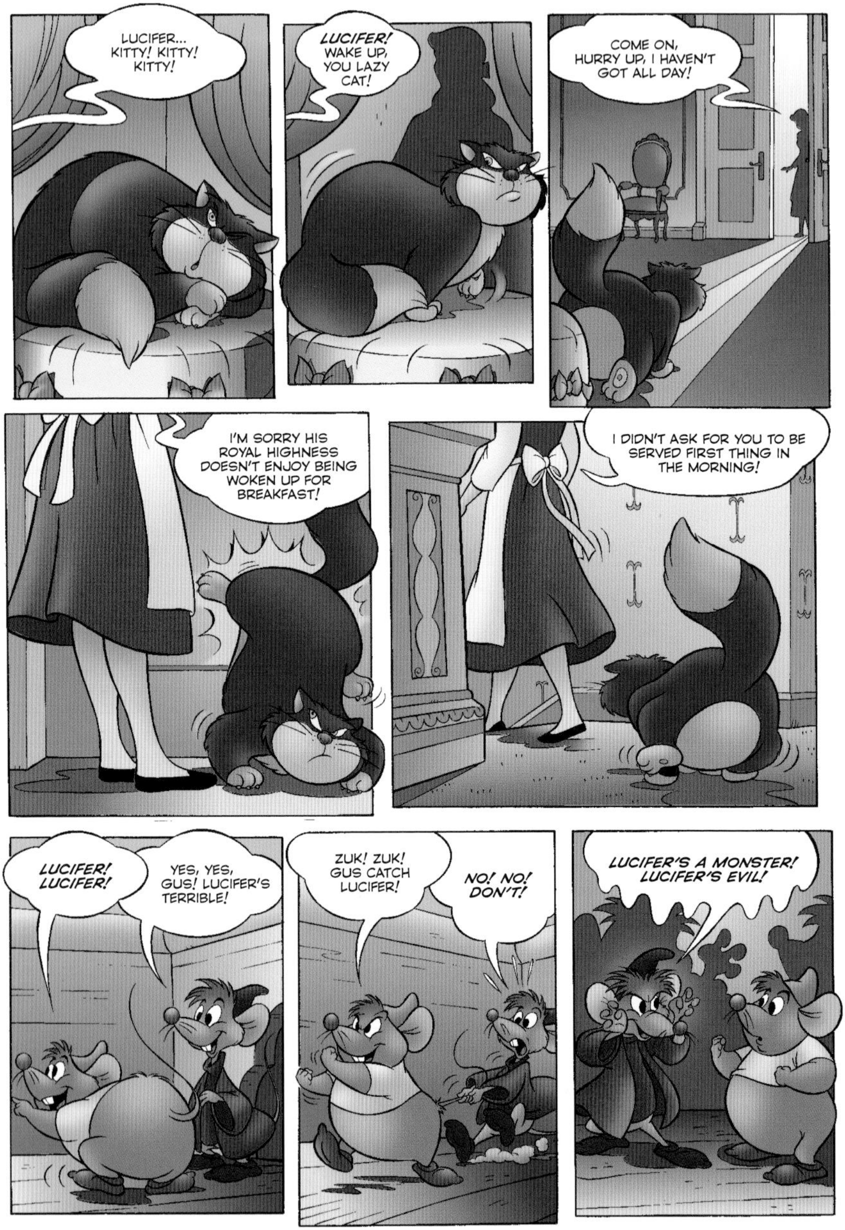
LUCIFER... KITTY! KITTY! KITTY!
LUCIFER! WAKE UP, YOU LAZY CAT!
COME ON, HURRY UP, I HAVEN'T GOT ALL DAY!
I'M SORRY HIS ROYAL HIGHNESS DOESN'T ENJOY BEING WOKEN UP FOR BREAKFAST!
I DIDN'T ASK FOR YOU TO BE SERVED FIRST THING IN THE MORNING!
LUCIFER! LUCIFER!
YES, YES, GUS! LUCIFER'S TERRIBLE!
ZUK! ZUK! GUS CATCH LUCIFER!
NO! NO! DON'T!
LUCIFER'S A MONSTER! LUCIFER'S EVIL!

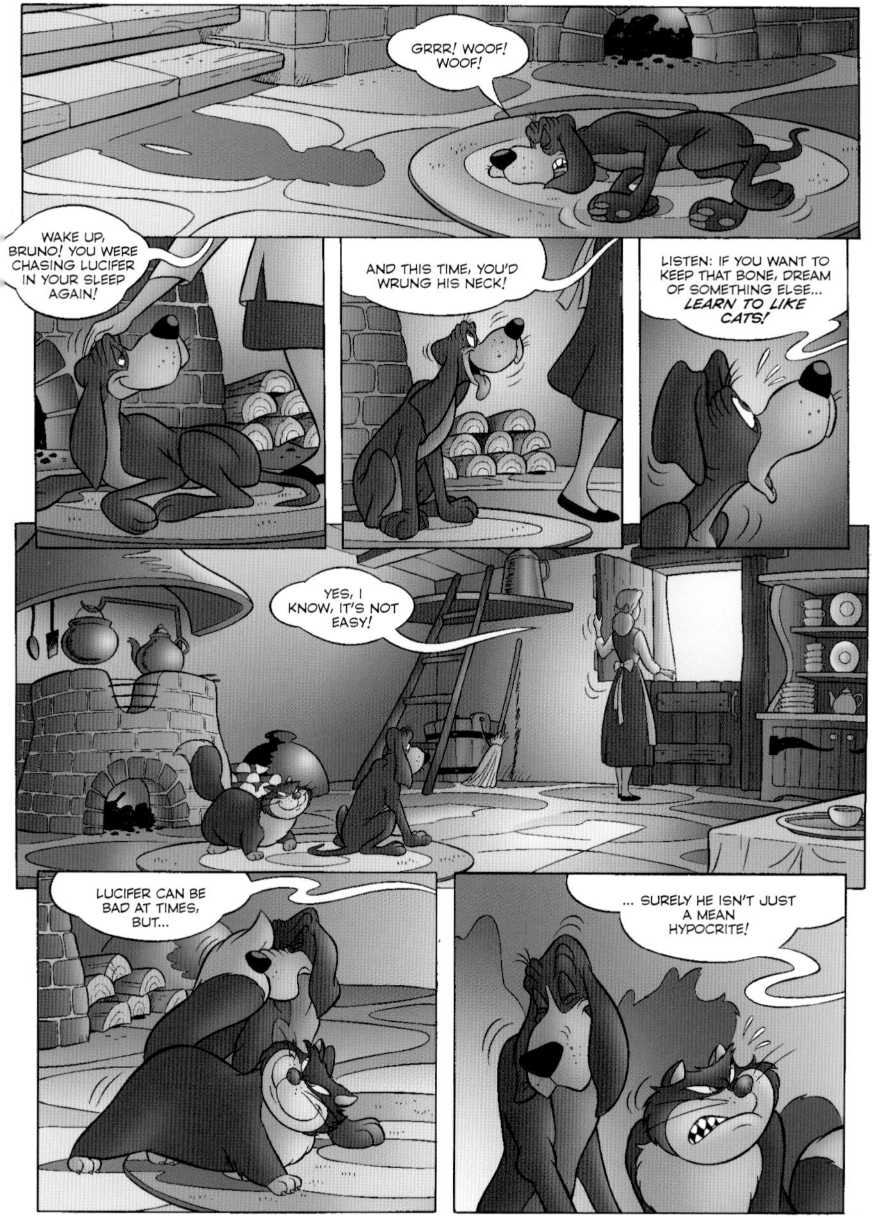
GRRR! WOOF! WOOF!
WAKE UP, BRUNO! YOU WERE CHASING LUCIFER IN YOUR SLEEP AGAIN!
AND THIS TIME, YOU'D WRUNG HIS NECK!
LISTEN: IF YOU WANT TO KEEP THAT BONE, DREAM OF SOMETHING ELSE... LEARN TO LIKE CATS!
YES, I KNOW, IT'S NOT EASY!
LUCIFER CAN BE BAD AT TIMES, BUT...
... SURELY HE ISN'T JUST A MEAN HYPOCRITE!

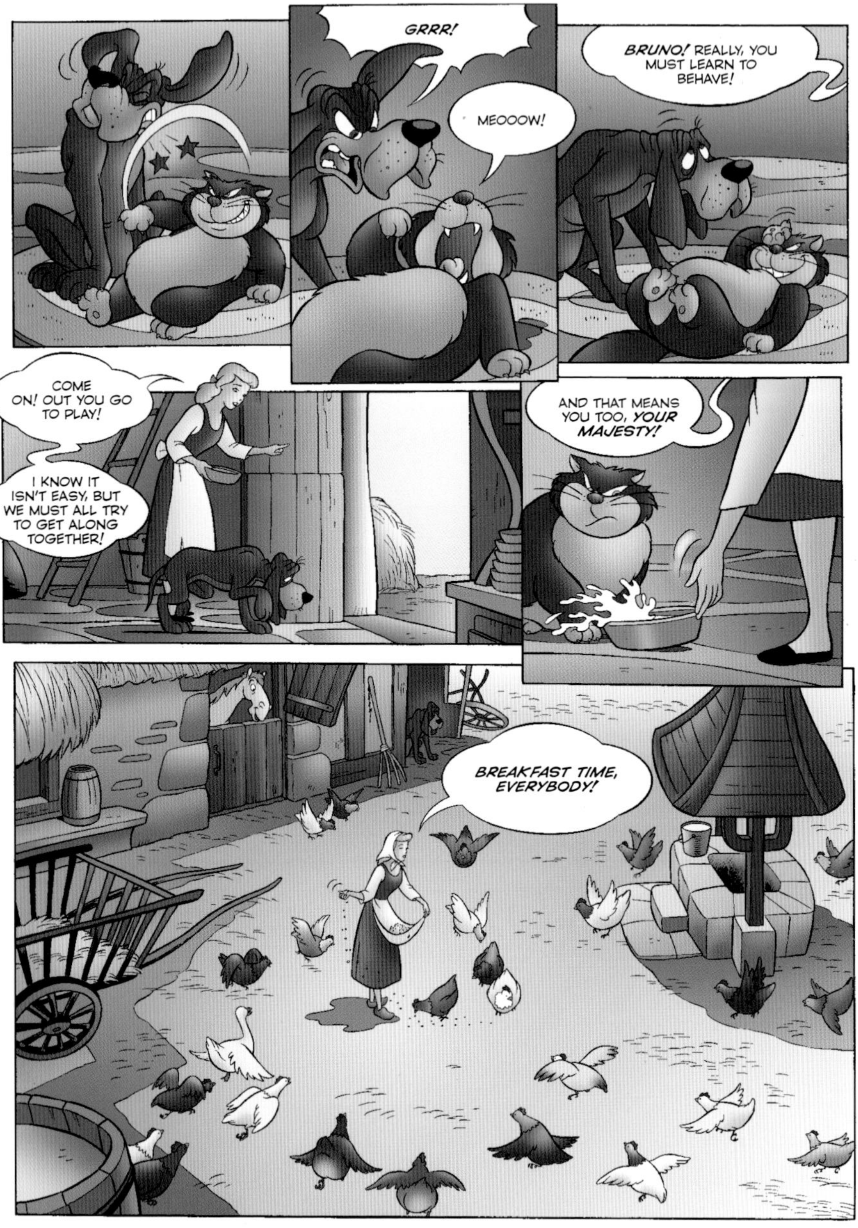
GRRR!
MEOOOW!
BRUNO! REALLY, YOU MUST LEARN TO BEHAVE!
COME ON! OUT YOU GO TO PLAY!
I KNOW IT ISN'T EASY, BUT WE MUST ALL TRY TO GET ALONG TOGETHER!
AND THAT MEANS YOU TOO, YOUR MAJESTY!
BREAKFAST TIME, EVERYBODY!

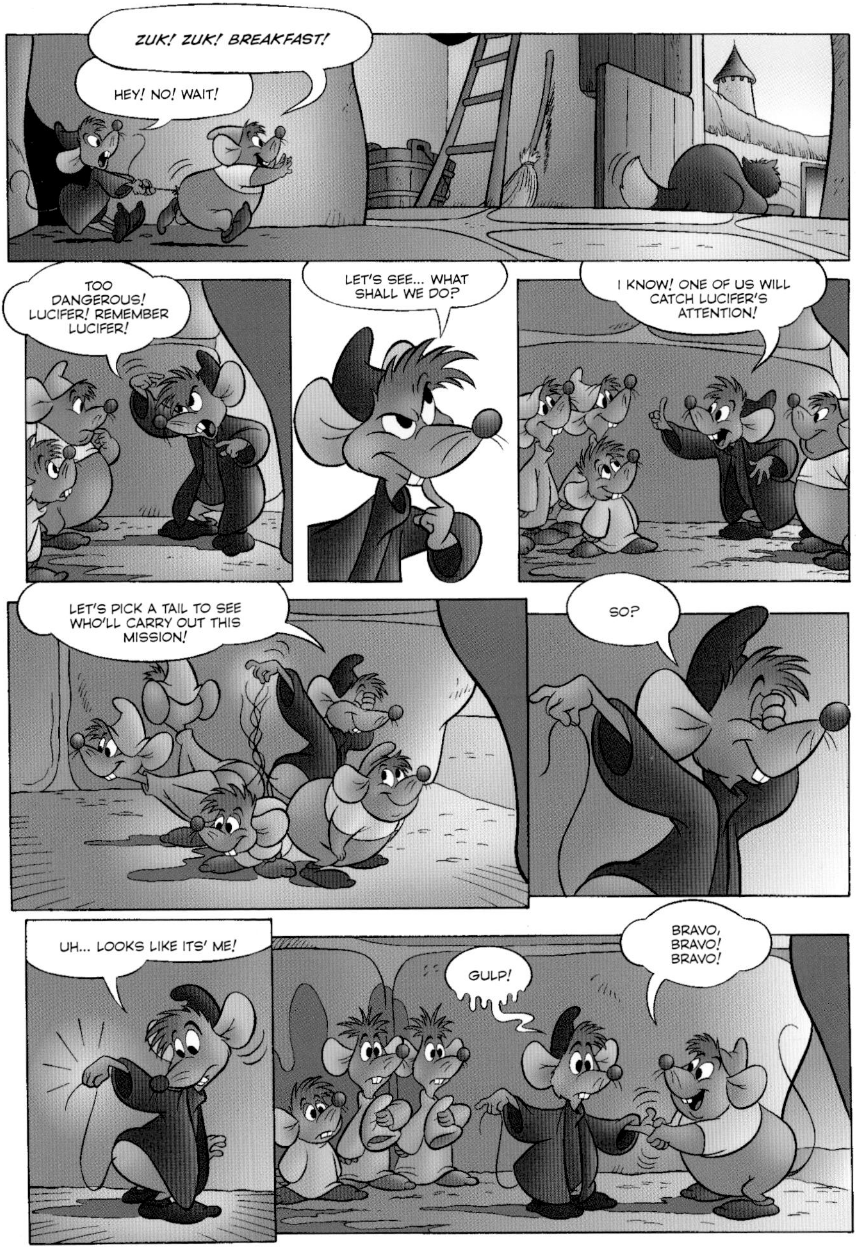
ZUK! ZUK! BREAKFAST!
HEY! NO! WAIT!
TOO DANGEROUS! LUCIFER! REMEMBER LUCIFER!
LET'S SEE... WHAT SHALL WE DO?
I KNOW! ONE OF US WILL CATCH LUCIFER'S ATTENTION!
LET'S PICK A TAIL TO SEE WHO'LL CARRY OUT THIS MISSION!
SO?
UH... LOOKS LIKE ITS' ME!
GULP!
BRAVO, BRAVO! BRAVO!

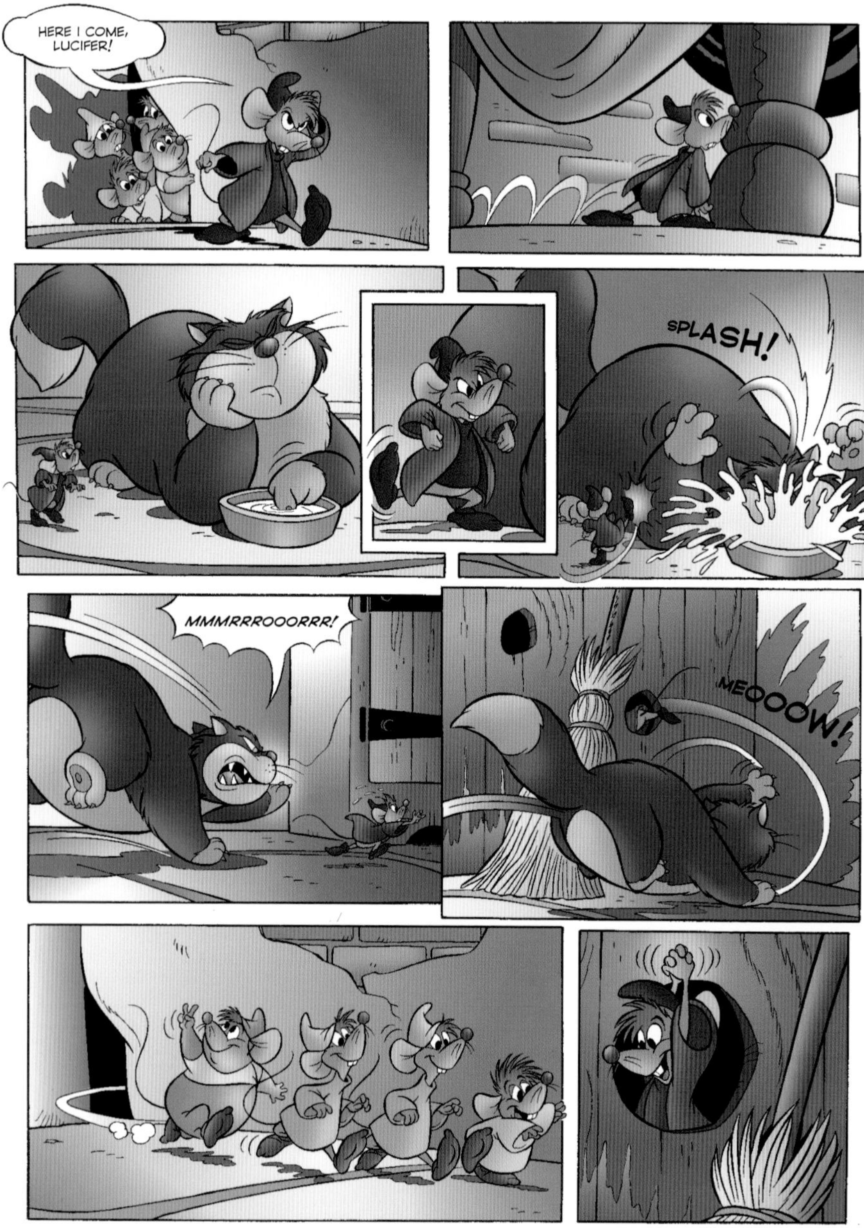
HERE I COME, LUCIFER!
SPLASH!
MMMRRROOORRR!
MEOOOW!

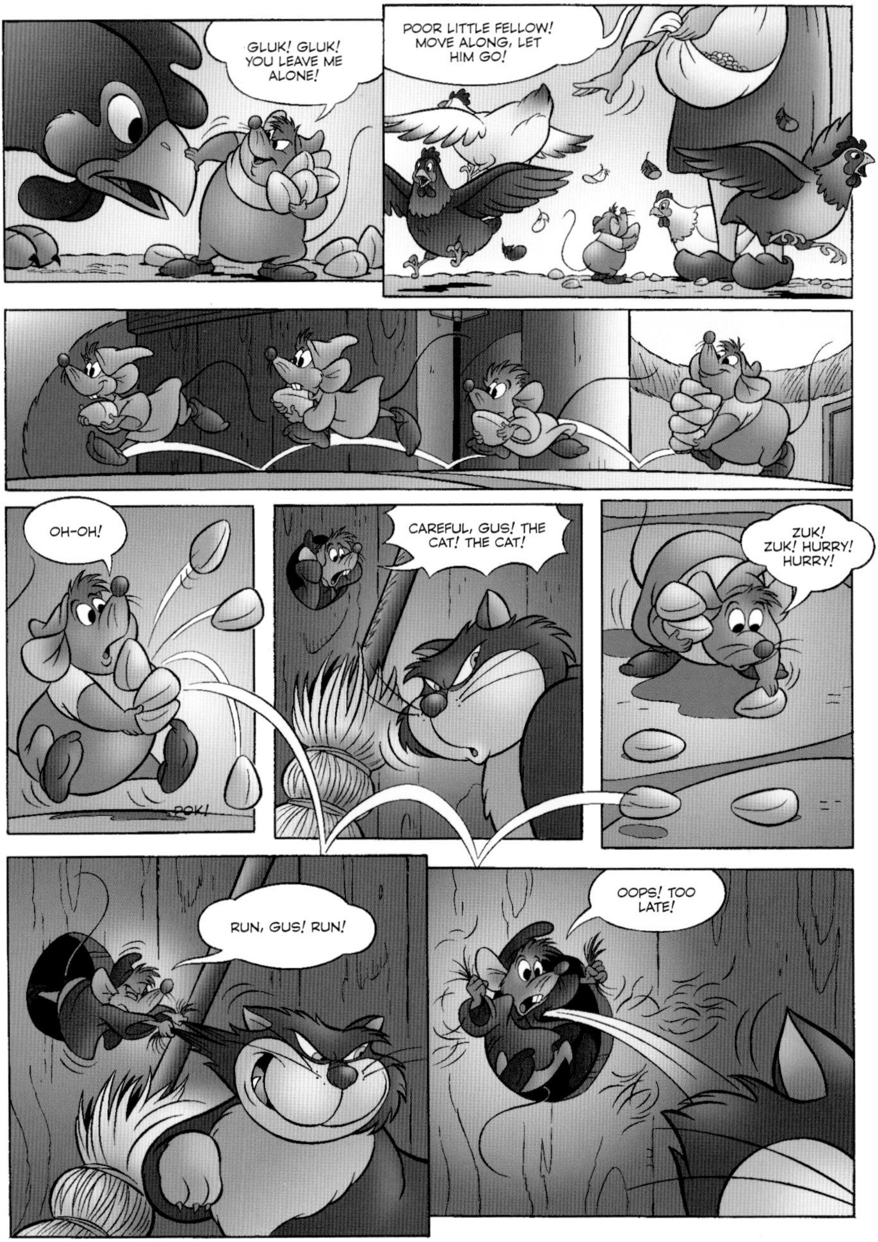
GLUK! GLUK! YOU LEAVE ME ALONE!
POOR LITTLE FELLOW! MOVE ALONG, LET HIM GO!
OH-OH!
POK!
CAREFUL, GUS! THE CAT! THE CAT!
ZUK! ZUK! HURRY! HURRY!
RUN, GUS! RUN!
OOPS! TOO LATE!

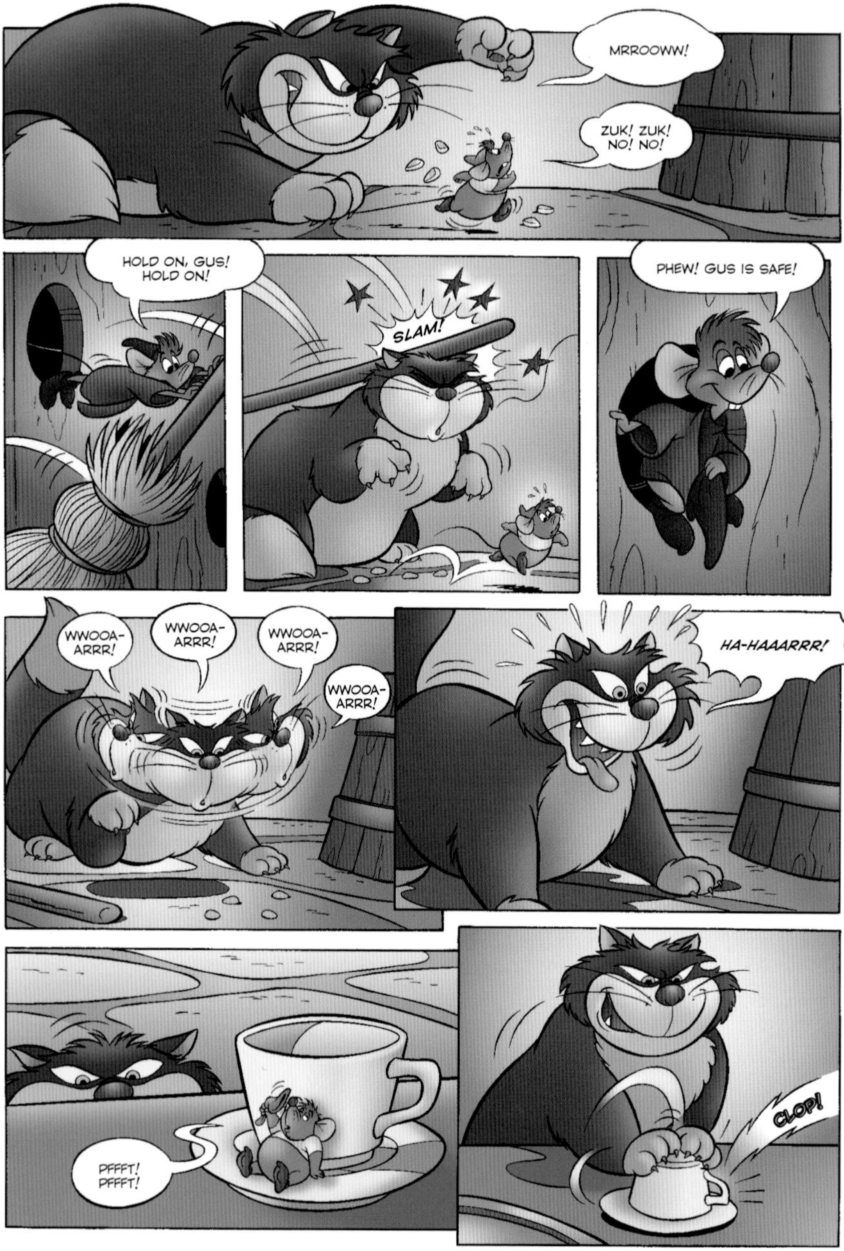
MRROOWW!
ZUK! ZUK! NO! NO!
HOLD ON, GUS! HOLD ON!
SLAM!
PHEW! GUS IS SAFE!
WWOOA-ARRR!
WWOOA-ARRR!
WWOOA-ARRR!
WWOOA-ARRR!
HA-HAAARRR!
PFFFT! PFFFT!
CLOP!

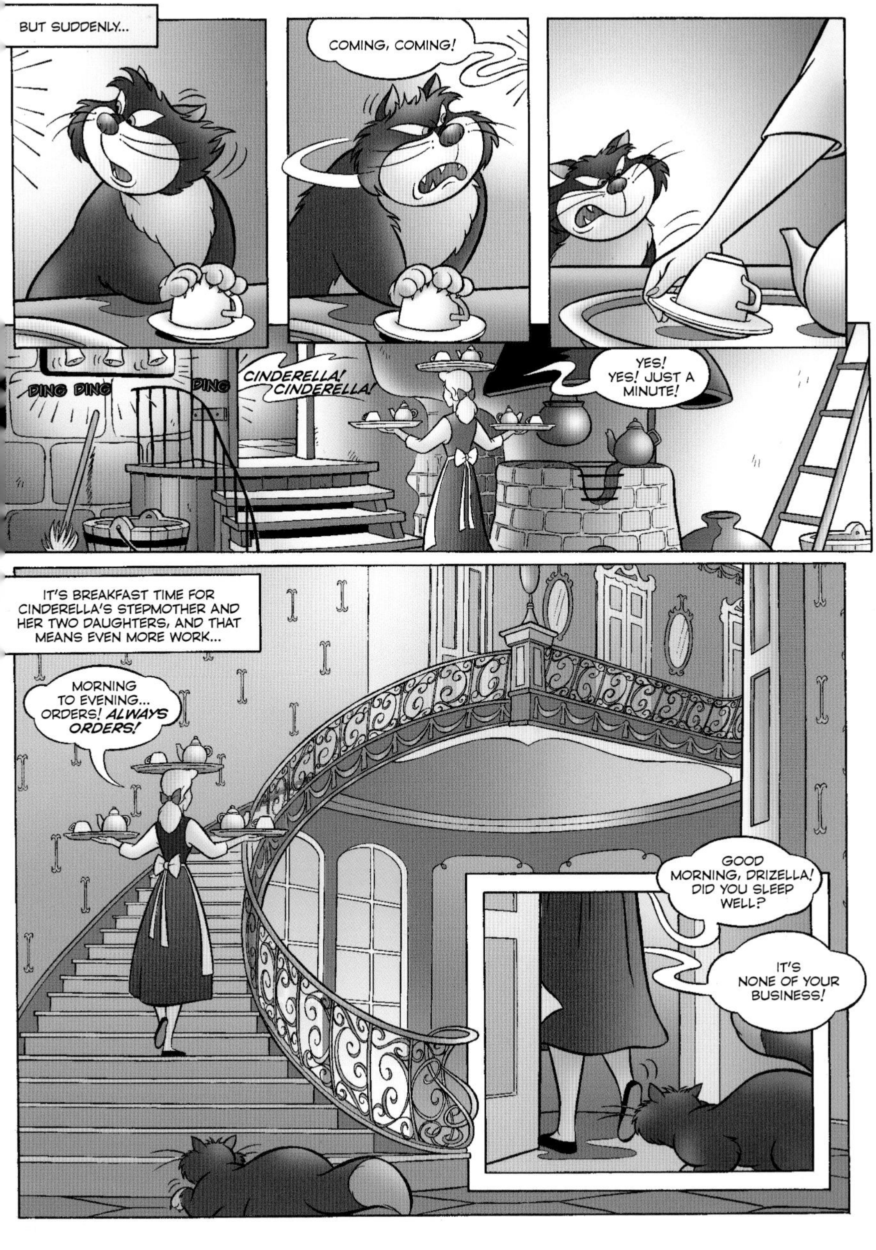
BUT SUDDENLY...
COMING, COMING!
DING DING
DING
CINDERELLA! CINDERELLA!
YES! YES! JUST A MINUTE!
IT'S BREAKFAST TIME FOR CINDERELLA'S STEPMOTHER AND HER TWO DAUGHTERS, AND THAT MEANS EVEN MORE WORK...
MORNING TO EVENING... ORDERS! ALWAYS ORDERS!
GOOD MORNING, DRIZELLA! DID YOU SLEEP WELL?
IT'S NONE OF YOUR BUSINESS!

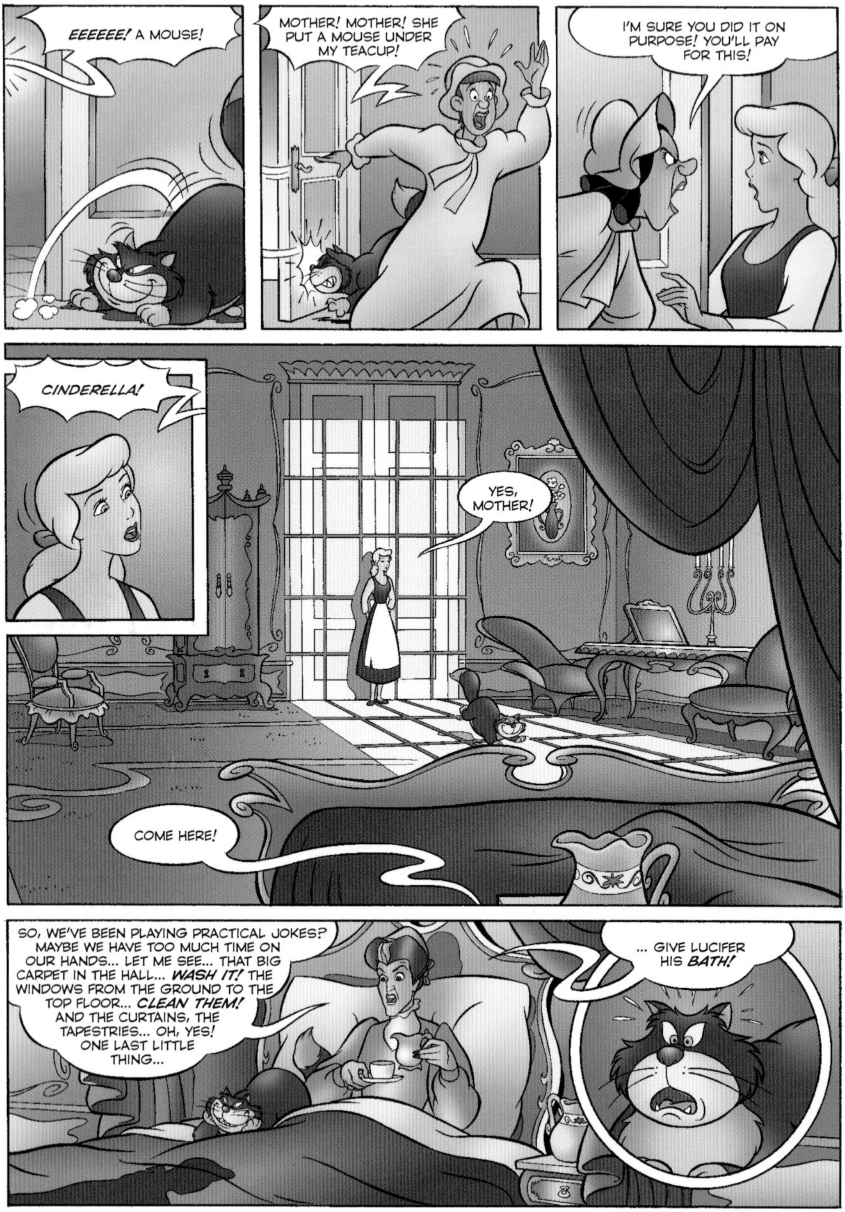
EEEEEE! A MOUSE!
MOTHER! MOTHER! SHE PUT A MOUSE UNDER MY TEACUP!
I'M SURE YOU DID IT ON PURPOSE! YOU'LL PAY FOR THIS!
CINDERELLA!
YES, MOTHER!
COME HERE!
SO, WE'VE BEEN PLAYING PRACTICAL JOKES? MAYBE WE HAVE TOO MUCH TIME ON OUR HANDS... LET ME SEE... THAT BIG CARPET IN THE HALL... WASH IT! THE WINDOWS FROM THE GROUND TO THE TOP FLOOR... CLEAN THEM! AND THE CURTAINS, THE TAPESTRIES... OH, YES! ONE LAST LITTLE THING...
... GIVE LUCIFER HIS BATH!

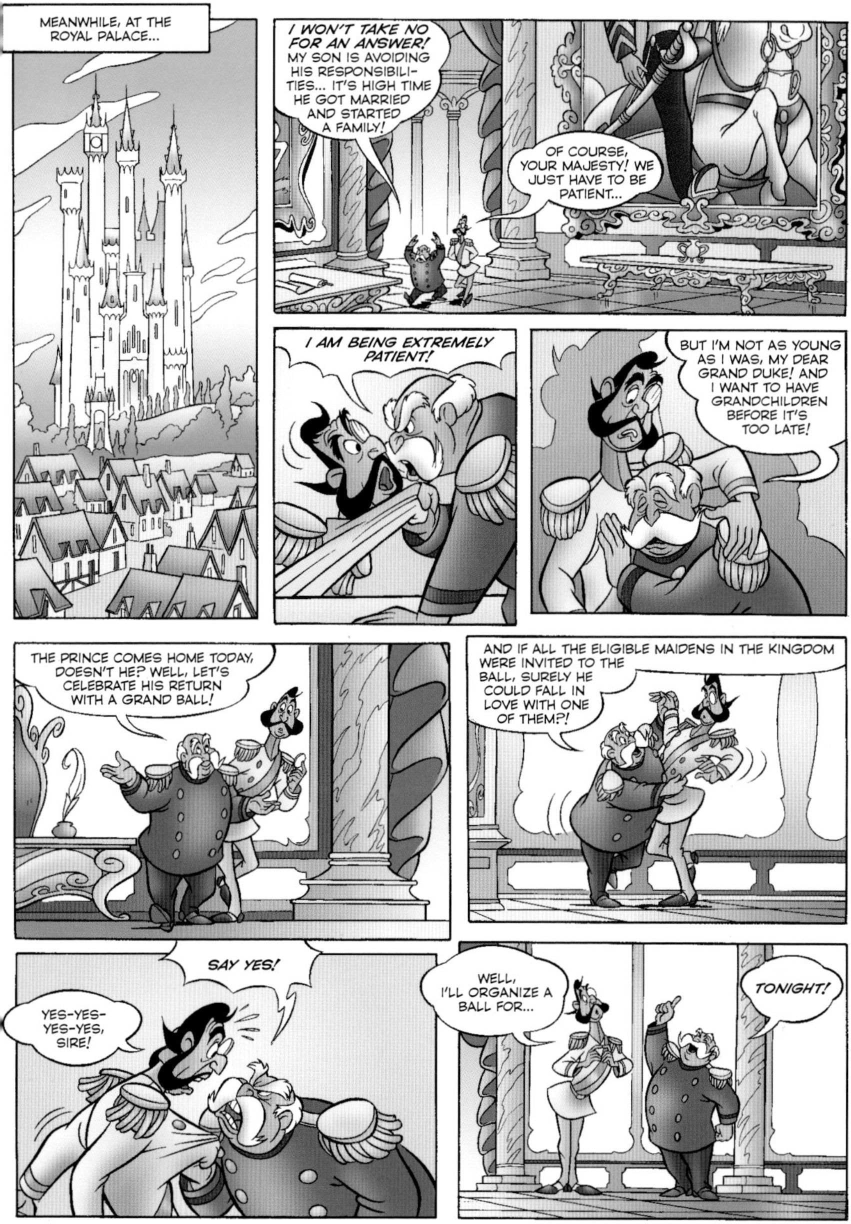
MEANWHILE, AT THE ROYAL PALACE...
I WON'T TAKE NO FOR AN ANSWER! MY SON IS AVOIDING HIS RESPONSIBILI- TIES... IT'S HIGH TIME HE GOT MARRIED AND STARTED A FAMILY!
OF COURSE, YOUR MAJESTY! WE JUST HAVE TO BE PATIENT...
I AM BEING EXTREMELY PATIENT!
BUT I'M NOT AS YOUNG AS I WAS, MY DEAR GRAND DUKE! AND I WANT TO HAVE GRANDCHILDREN BEFORE IT'S TOO LATE!
THE PRINCE COMES HOME TODAY, DOESN'T HE? WELL, LET'S CELEBRATE HIS RETURN WITH A GRAND BALL!
AND IF ALL THE ELIGIBLE MAIDENS IN THE KINGDOM WERE INVITED TO THE BALL, SURELY HE COULD FALL IN LOVE WITH ONE OF THEM?!
SAY YES!
YES-YES-YES-YES, SIRE!
WELL, I'LL ORGANIZE A BALL FOR...
TONIGHT!

AN URGENT MESSAGE FROM HIS MAJESTY!

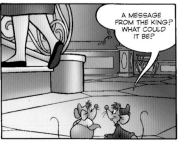

A MESSAGE FROM THE KING?! WHAT COULD IT BE?

CINDERELLA! I THOUGHT I TOLD YOU NEVER TO INTERRUPT US!

BUT... A LETTER HAS JUST COME FROM THE PALACE!

THE PALACE?!

GIVE IT TO ME! QUICK!

LISTEN! THERE'S GOING TO BE A BALL IN THE PRINCE'S HONOR AND ALL THE ELIGIBLE MAIDENS IN THE KINGDOM ARE INVITED!

HOW WONDERFUL! I'M JUST MEANT TO BE A PRINCESS!

BUT... THAT MEANS I CAN GO TOO!

HEE! HEE! CAN YOU SEE HER DANCING WITH THE PRINCE?

VERY HONORED, YOUR HIGHNESS! YOU WILL HOLD MY BROOM!

BUT... WHY NOT? AFTER ALL, I'M PART OF THE FAMILY!

WHY SHOULDN'T YOU GO, AFTER ALL? AS LONG AS YOU'VE FINISHED ALL YOUR CHORES... AND IF YOU HAVE A SUITABLE DRESS TO WEAR!

THANK YOU, MOTHER!

MOTHER! DO YOU REALIZE WHAT YOU'VE SAID?

YES, OF COURSE...

... I SAID: IF...

OH! SO YOU DID!

HEE! HEE! HEE!

CINDERELLA'S TOO HAPPY TO REALIZE HER STEPMOTHER HAS TRICKED HER...

LOOK AT THIS LOVELY DRESS! IT BELONGED TO MY MOTHER!

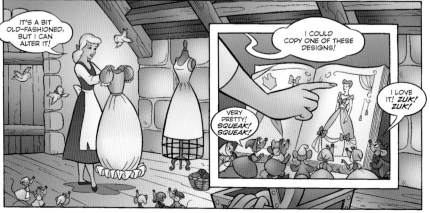

IT'S A BIT OLD-FASHIONED, BUT I CAN ALTER IT!

I COULD COPY ONE OF THESE DESIGNS!

VERY PRETTY! SQUEAK! SQUEAK!

I LOVE IT! ZUK! ZUK!

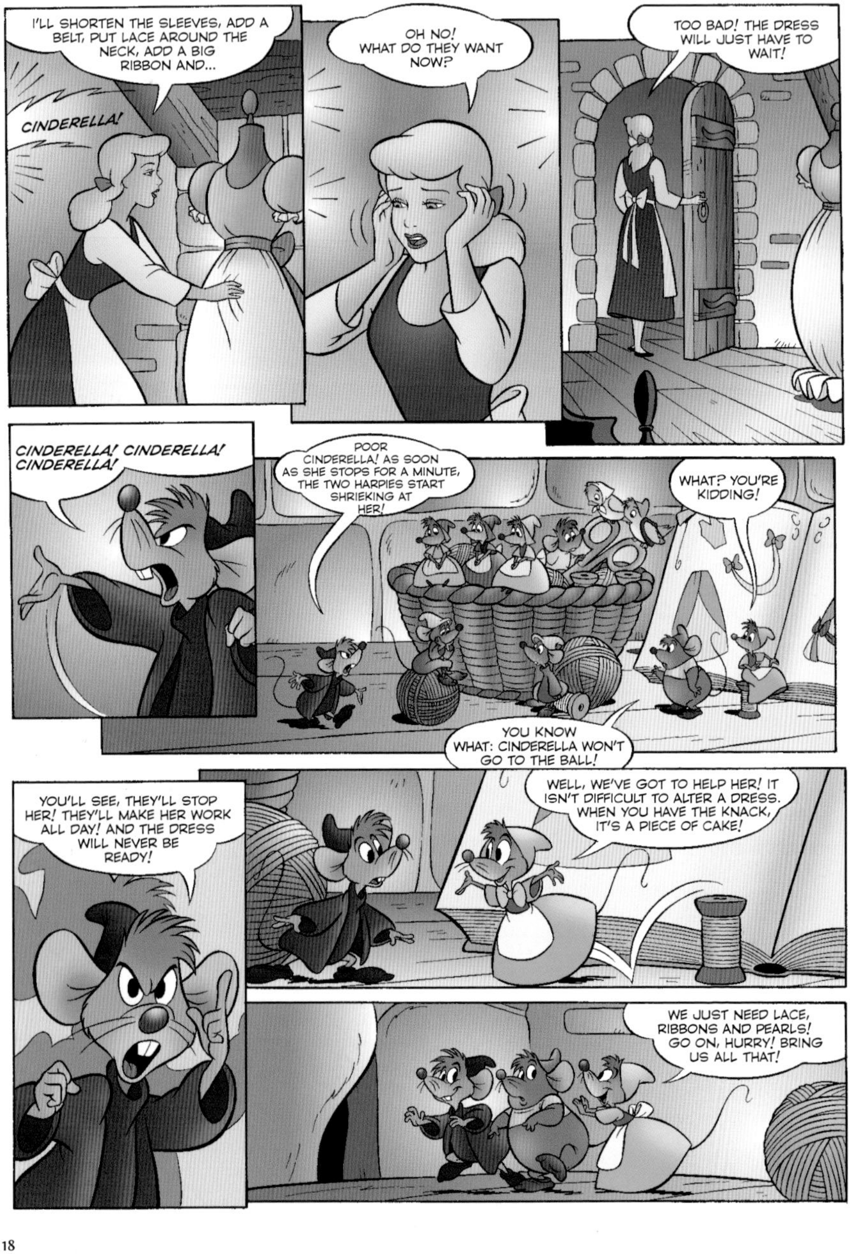
I'LL SHORTEN THE SLEEVES, ADD A BELT, PUT LACE AROUND THE NECK, ADD A BIG RIBBON AND...
CINDERELLA!
OH NO! WHAT DO THEY WANT NOW?
TOO BAD! THE DRESS WILL JUST HAVE TO WAIT!
CINDERELLA! CINDERELLA! CINDERELLA!
POOR CINDERELLA! AS SOON AS SHE STOPS FOR A MINUTE, THE TWO HARPIES START SHRIEKING AT HER!
WHAT? YOU'RE KIDDING!
YOU KNOW WHAT: CINDERELLA WON'T GO TO THE BALL!
YOU'LL SEE, THEY'LL STOP HER! THEY'LL MAKE HER WORK ALL DAY! AND THE DRESS WILL NEVER BE READY!
WELL, WE'VE GOT TO HELP HER! IT ISN'T DIFFICULT TO ALTER A DRESS. WHEN YOU HAVE THE KNACK, IT'S A PIECE OF CAKE!
WE JUST NEED LACE, RIBBONS AND PEARLS! GO ON, HURRY! BRING US ALL THAT!

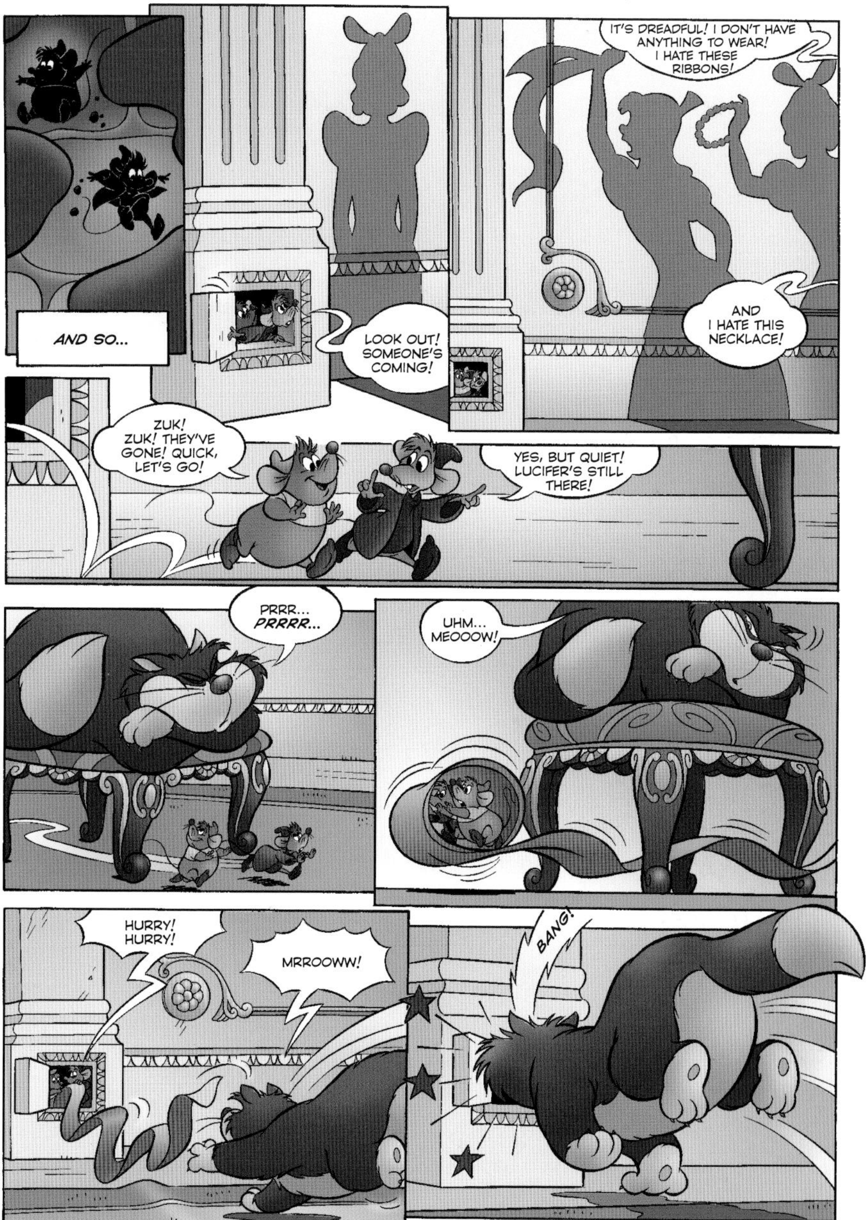
AND SO...
LOOK OUT! SOMEONE'S COMING!
IT'S DREADFUL! I DON'T HAVE ANYTHING TO WEAR! I HATE THESE RIBBONS!
AND I HATE THIS NECKLACE!
ZUK! ZUK! THEY'VE GONE! QUICK, LET'S GO!
YES, BUT QUIET! LUCIFER'S STILL THERE!
PRRR... PRRRR...
UHM... MEOOOW!
HURRY! HURRY!
MRROOWW!
BANG!

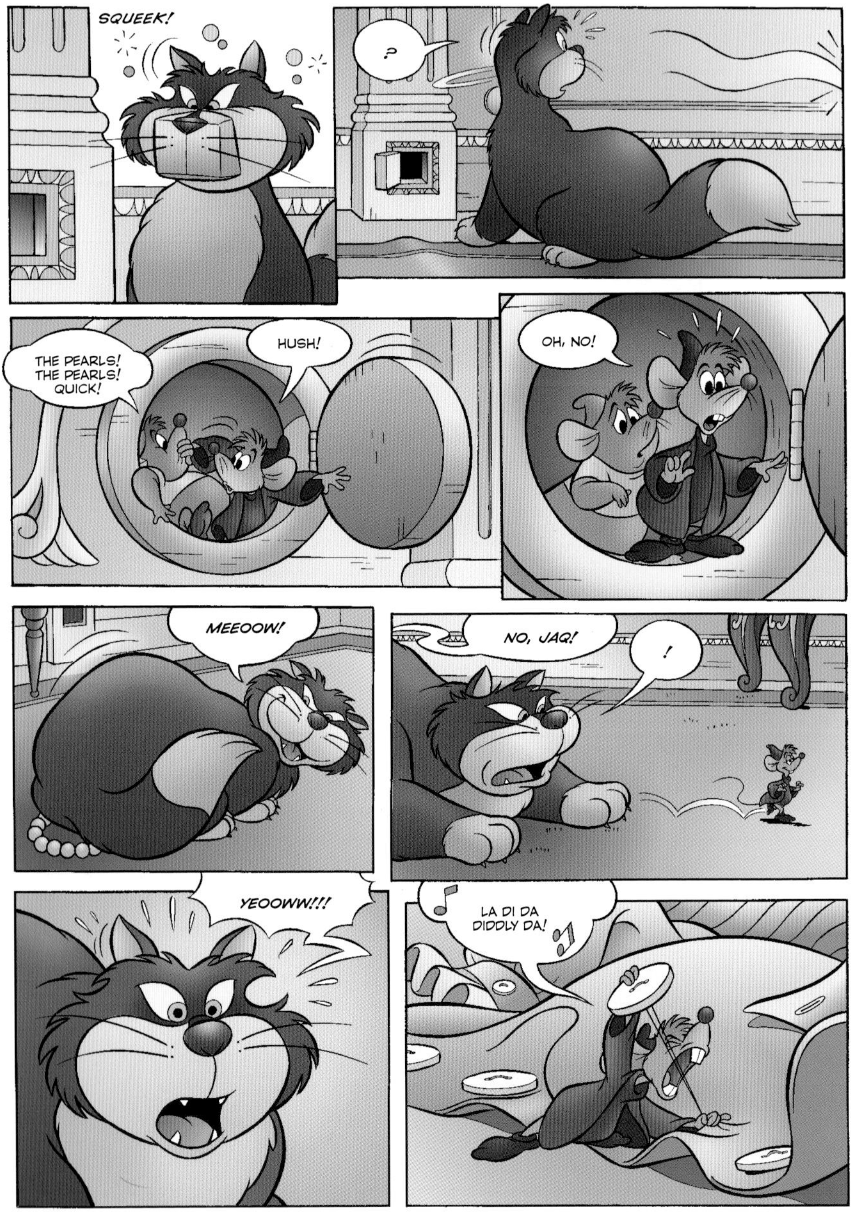
SQUEEK!
?
THE PEARLS! THE PEARLS! QUICK!
HUSH!
OH, NO!
MEEOOW!
NO, JAQ!
!
YEOOWW!!!
LA DI DA DIDDLY DA!

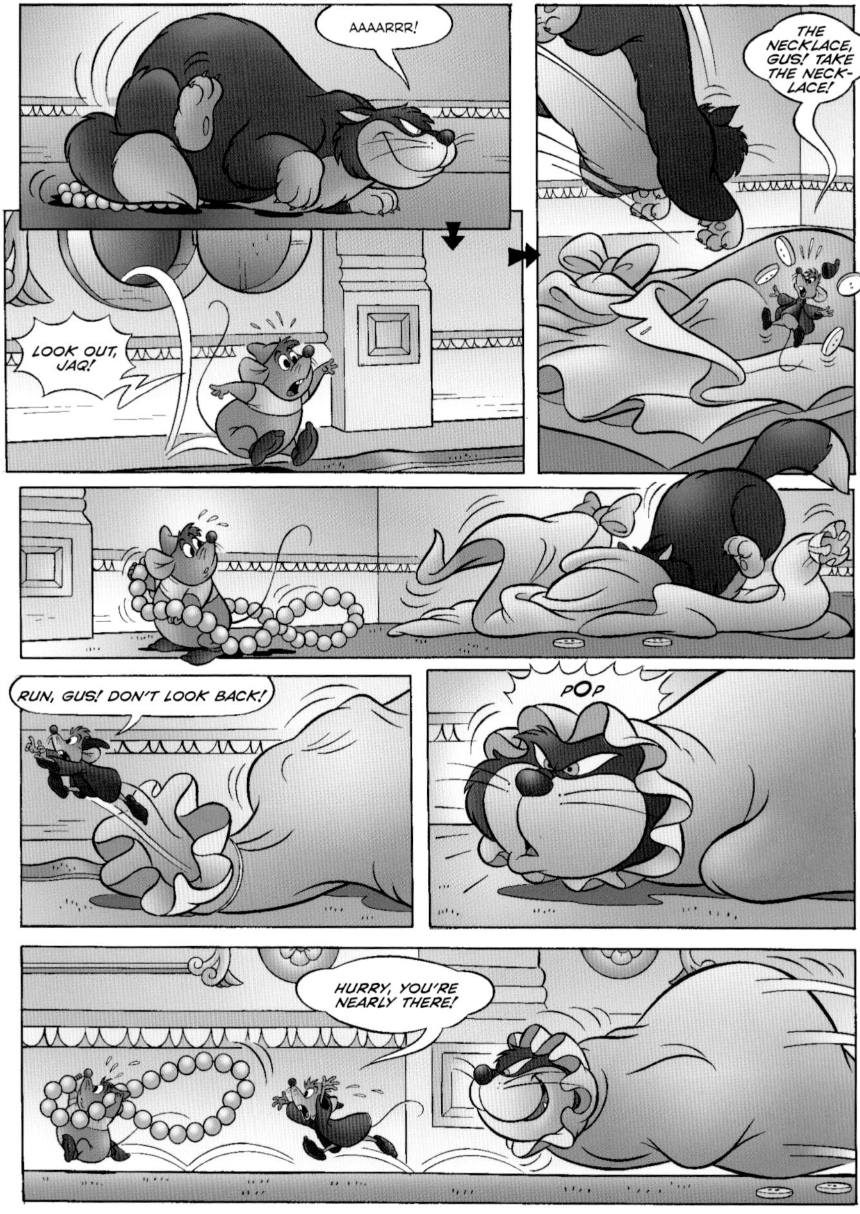
AAAARRR!
LOOK OUT, JAQ!
THE NECKLACE, GUS! TAKE THE NECK-LACE!
RUN, GUS! DON'T LOOK BACK!
POP
HURRY, YOU'RE NEARLY THERE!

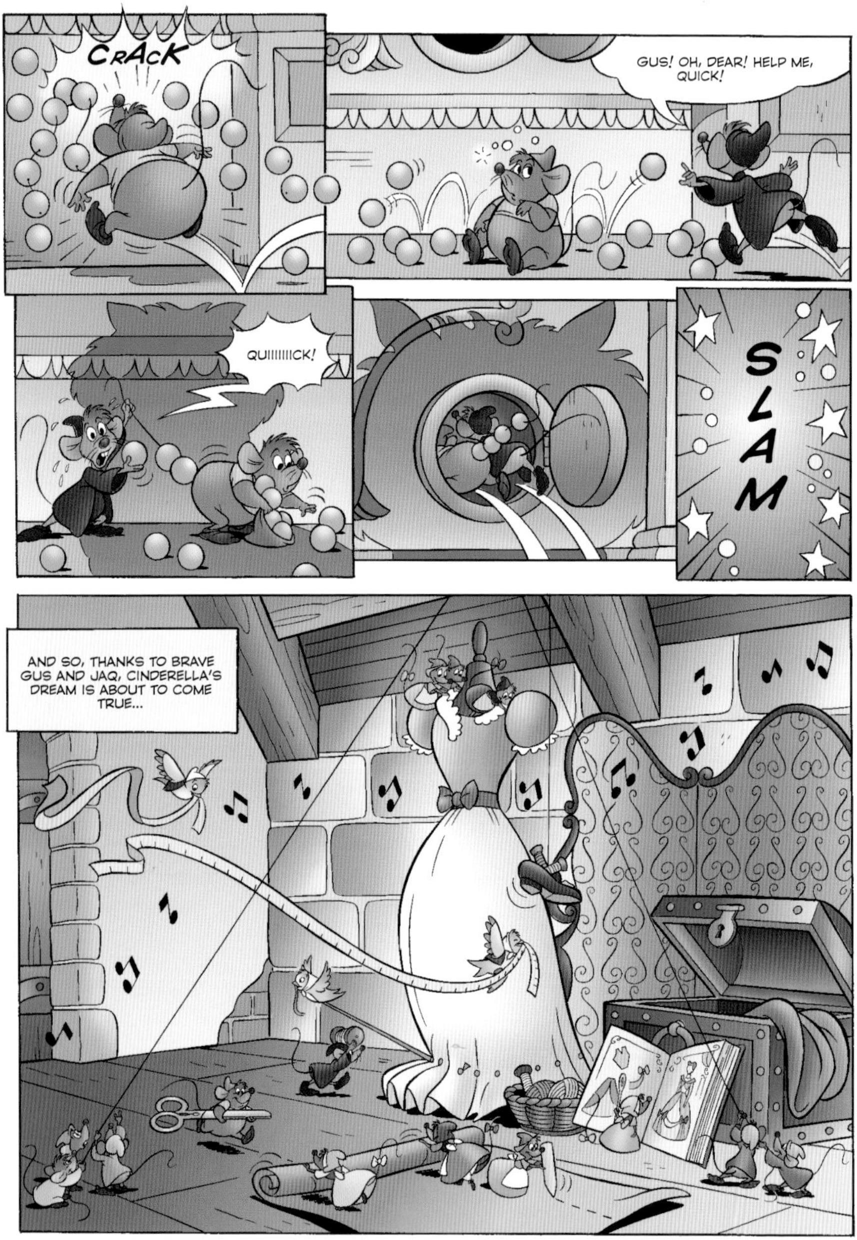
CRACK
GUS! OH, DEAR! HELP ME, QUICK!
QUIIIIIIICK!
SLAM
AND SO, THANKS TO BRAVE GUS AND JAQ, CINDERELLA'S DREAM IS ABOUT TO COME TRUE...

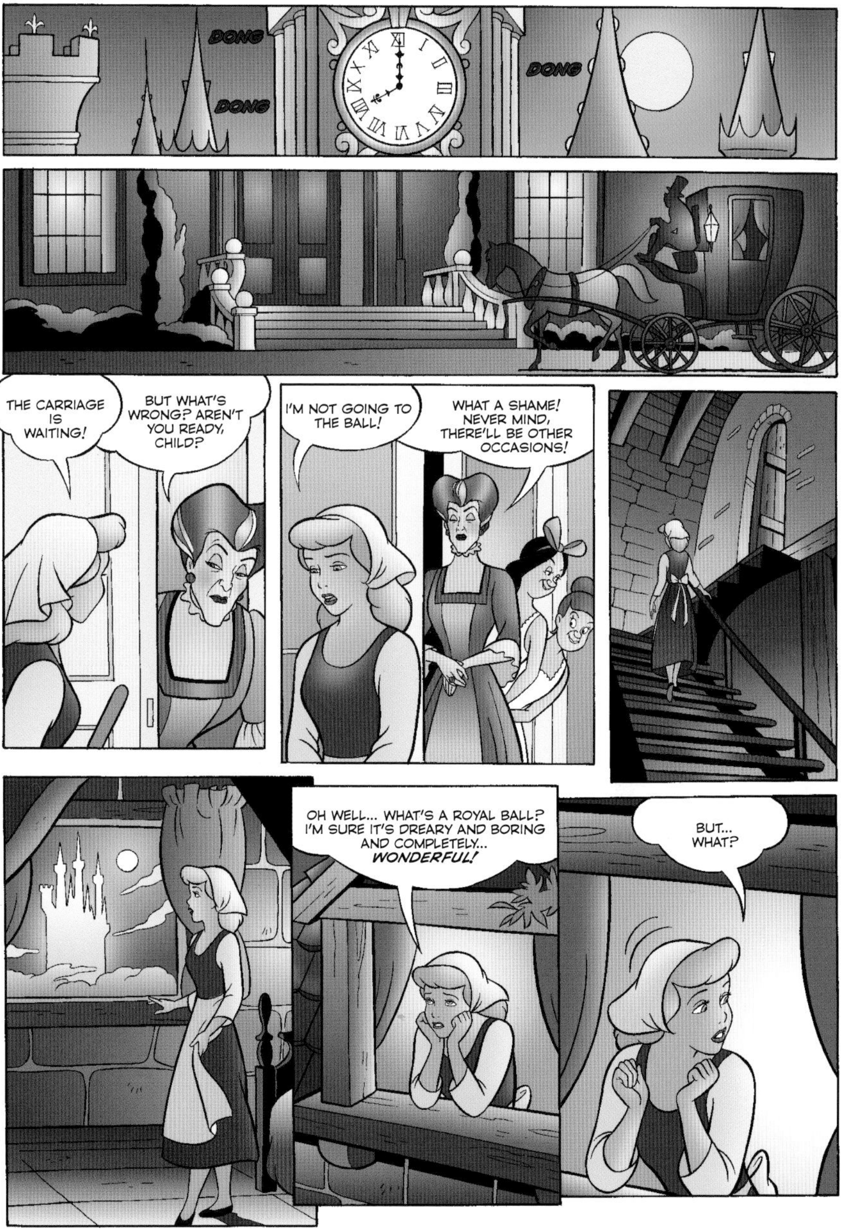
DONG
DONG
DONG
DONG
THE CARRIAGE IS WAITING!
BUT WHAT'S WRONG? AREN'T YOU READY, CHILD?
I'M NOT GOING TO THE BALL!
WHAT A SHAME! NEVER MIND, THERE'LL BE OTHER OCCASIONS!
OH WELL... WHAT'S A ROYAL BALL? I'M SURE IT'S DREARY AND BORING AND COMPLETELY... *WONDERFUL!*
BUT... WHAT?

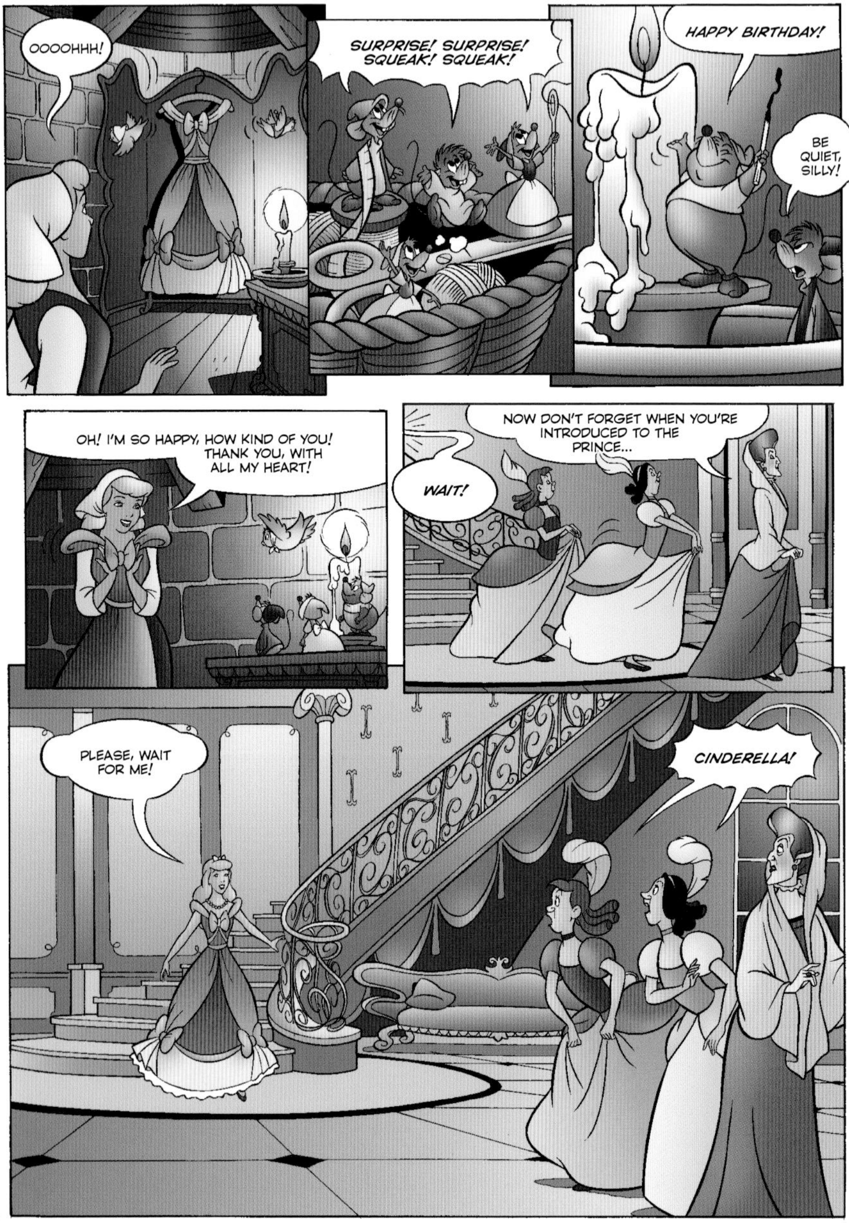
OOOOHHH!
SURPRISE! SURPRISE! SQUEAK! SQUEAK!
HAPPY BIRTHDAY!
BE QUIET, SILLY!
OH! I'M SO HAPPY, HOW KIND OF YOU! THANK YOU, WITH ALL MY HEART!
NOW DON'T FORGET WHEN YOU'RE INTRODUCED TO THE PRINCE...
WAIT!
PLEASE, WAIT FOR ME!
CINDERELLA!

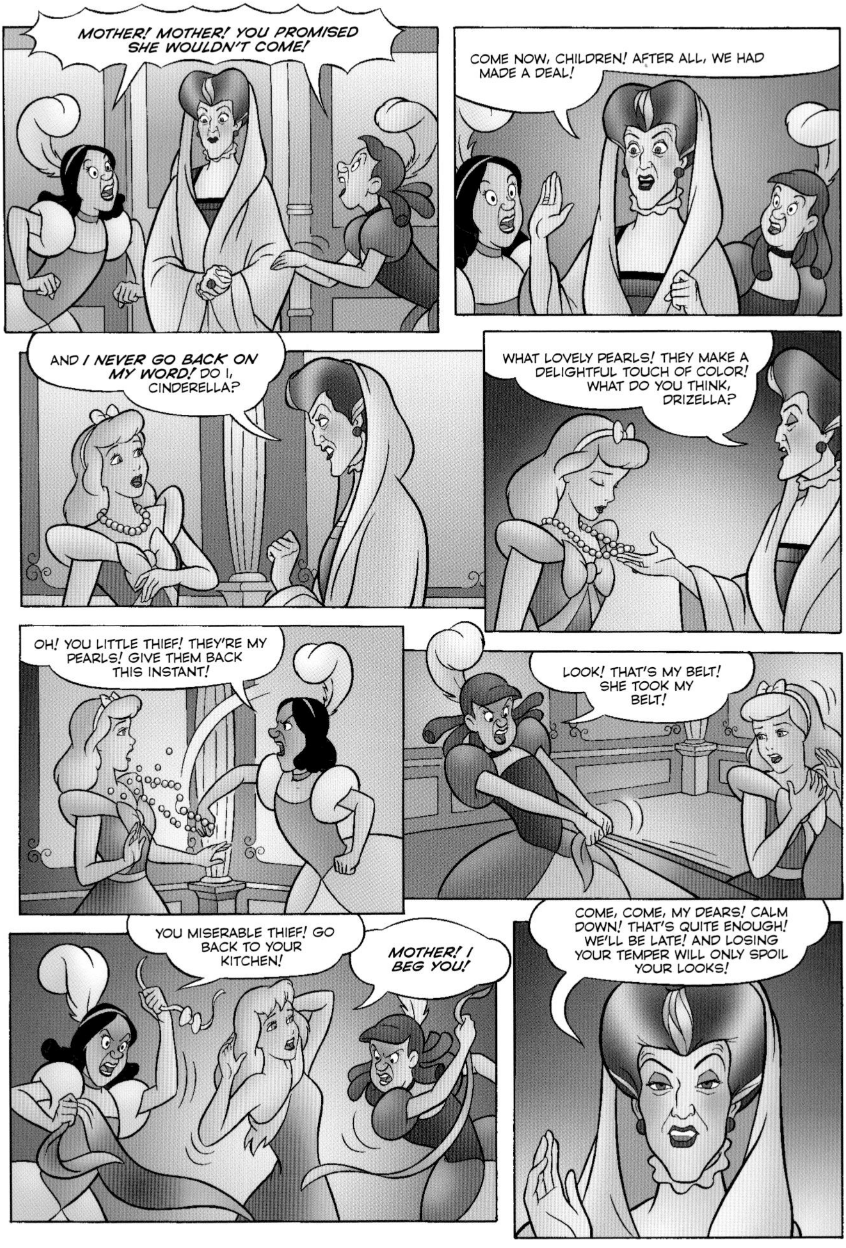
MOTHER! MOTHER! YOU PROMISED SHE WOULDN'T COME!
COME NOW, CHILDREN! AFTER ALL, WE HAD MADE A DEAL!
AND I NEVER GO BACK ON MY WORD! DO I, CINDERELLA?
WHAT LOVELY PEARLS! THEY MAKE A DELIGHTFUL TOUCH OF COLOR! WHAT DO YOU THINK, DRIZELLA?
OH! YOU LITTLE THIEF! THEY'RE MY PEARLS! GIVE THEM BACK THIS INSTANT!
LOOK! THAT'S MY BELT! SHE TOOK MY BELT!
YOU MISERABLE THIEF! GO BACK TO YOUR KITCHEN!
MOTHER! I BEG YOU!
COME, COME, MY DEARS! CALM DOWN! THAT'S QUITE ENOUGH! WE'LL BE LATE! AND LOSING YOUR TEMPER WILL ONLY SPOIL YOUR LOOKS!

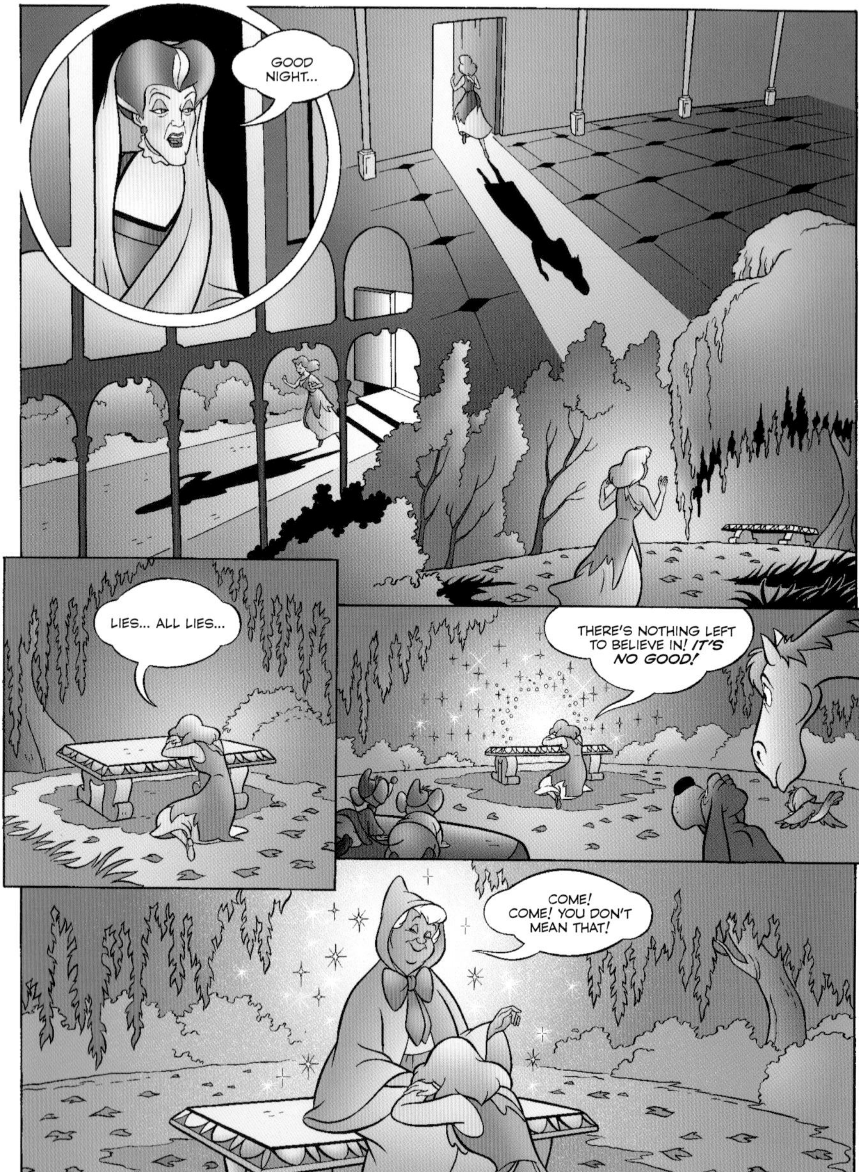
GOOD NIGHT...
LIES... ALL LIES...
THERE'S NOTHING LEFT TO BELIEVE IN! *IT'S NO GOOD!*
COME! COME! YOU DON'T MEAN THAT!

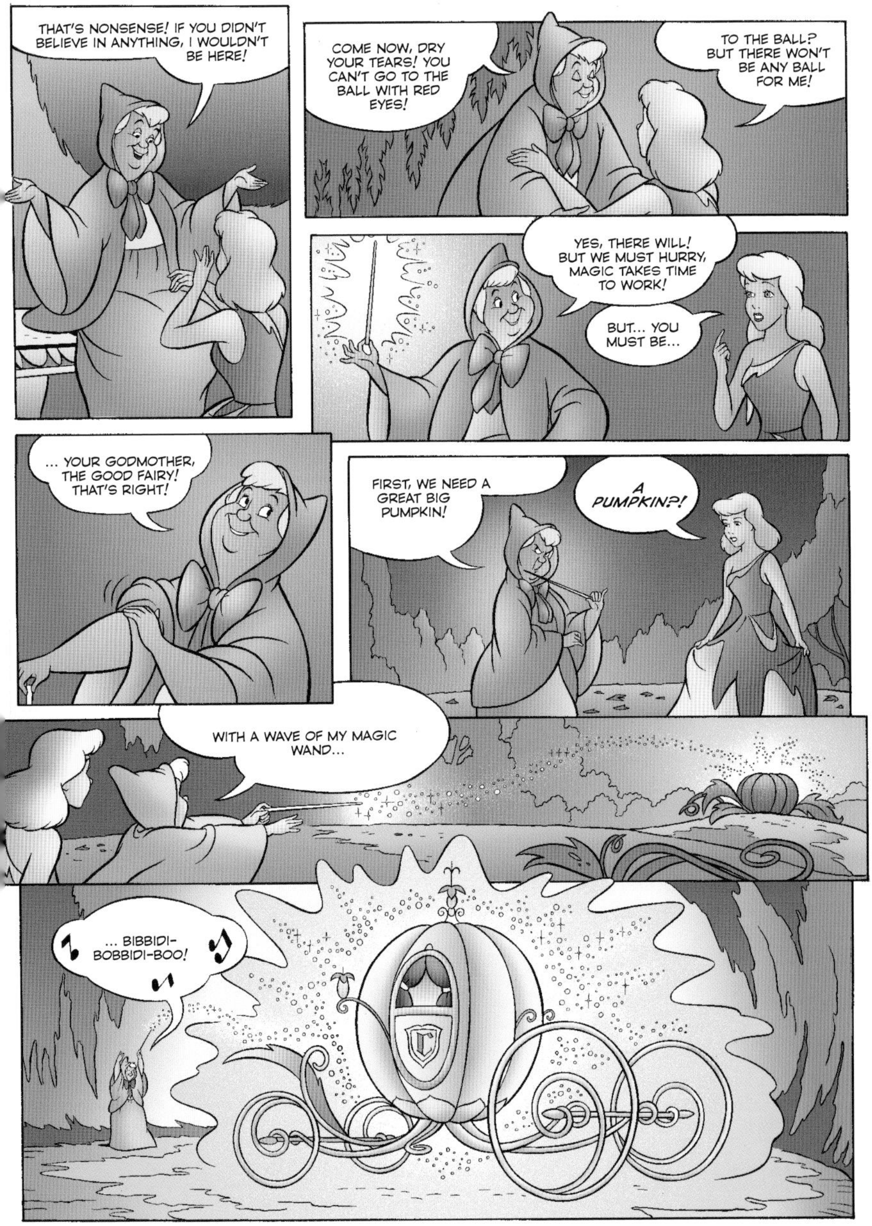
THAT'S NONSENSE! IF YOU DIDN'T BELIEVE IN ANYTHING, I WOULDN'T BE HERE!
COME NOW, DRY YOUR TEARS! YOU CAN'T GO TO THE BALL WITH RED EYES!
TO THE BALL? BUT THERE WON'T BE ANY BALL FOR ME!
YES, THERE WILL! BUT WE MUST HURRY, MAGIC TAKES TIME TO WORK!
BUT... YOU MUST BE...
... YOUR GODMOTHER, THE GOOD FAIRY! THAT'S RIGHT!
FIRST, WE NEED A GREAT BIG PUMPKIN!
A PUMPKIN?!
WITH A WAVE OF MY MAGIC WAND...
... BIBBIDI-BOBBIDI-BOO!

FOR SUCH AN ELEGANT CARRIAGE, WE NEED... MICE!

MICE?

HA! SWEET LITTLE THINGS! PERFECT!

BIBBIDI-BOBBIDI-BOO!

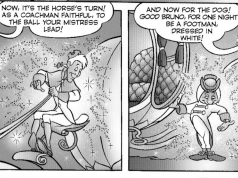

NOW, IT'S THE HORSE'S TURN! AS A COACHMAN FAITHFUL, TO THE BALL YOUR MISTRESS LEAD!

AND NOW FOR THE DOG! GOOD BRUNO, FOR ONE NIGHT BE A FOOTMAN, DRESSED IN WHITE!

EXCUSE ME, BUT DON'T YOU THINK MY DRESS...

OOOOH! GOOD HEAVENS, MY DEAR, JUST LOOK AT THOSE RAGS!

WHAT WAS I THINKING OF? BIBBIDI-BOBBIDI-BOO!

NOW, CINDERELLA, REMEMBER! ON THE LAST STROKE OF MIDNIGHT, THE SPELL WILL BE BROKEN AND EVERYTHING WILL BE AS BEFORE. HURRY! THE BALL IS WAITING AND TIME WILL FLY!

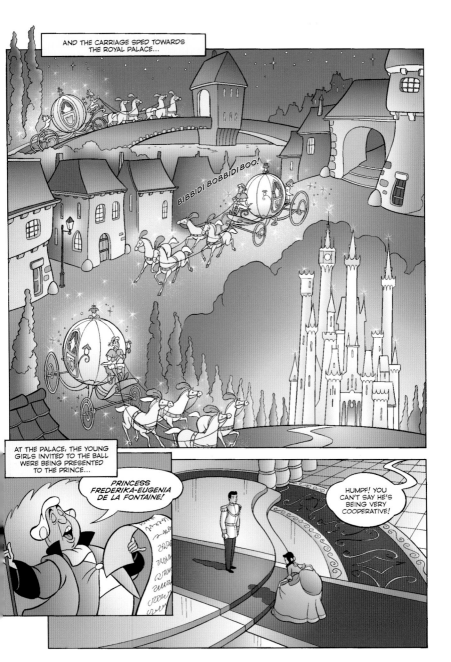

AND THE CARRIAGE SPED TOWARDS THE ROYAL PALACE...

BIBBIDI BOBBIDI BOO!

AT THE PALACE, THE YOUNG GIRLS INVITED TO THE BALL WERE BEING PRESENTED TO THE PRINCE...

PRINCESS FREDERIKA-EUGENIA DE LA FONTAINE!

HUMPF! YOU CAN'T SAY HE'S BEING VERY COOPERATIVE!

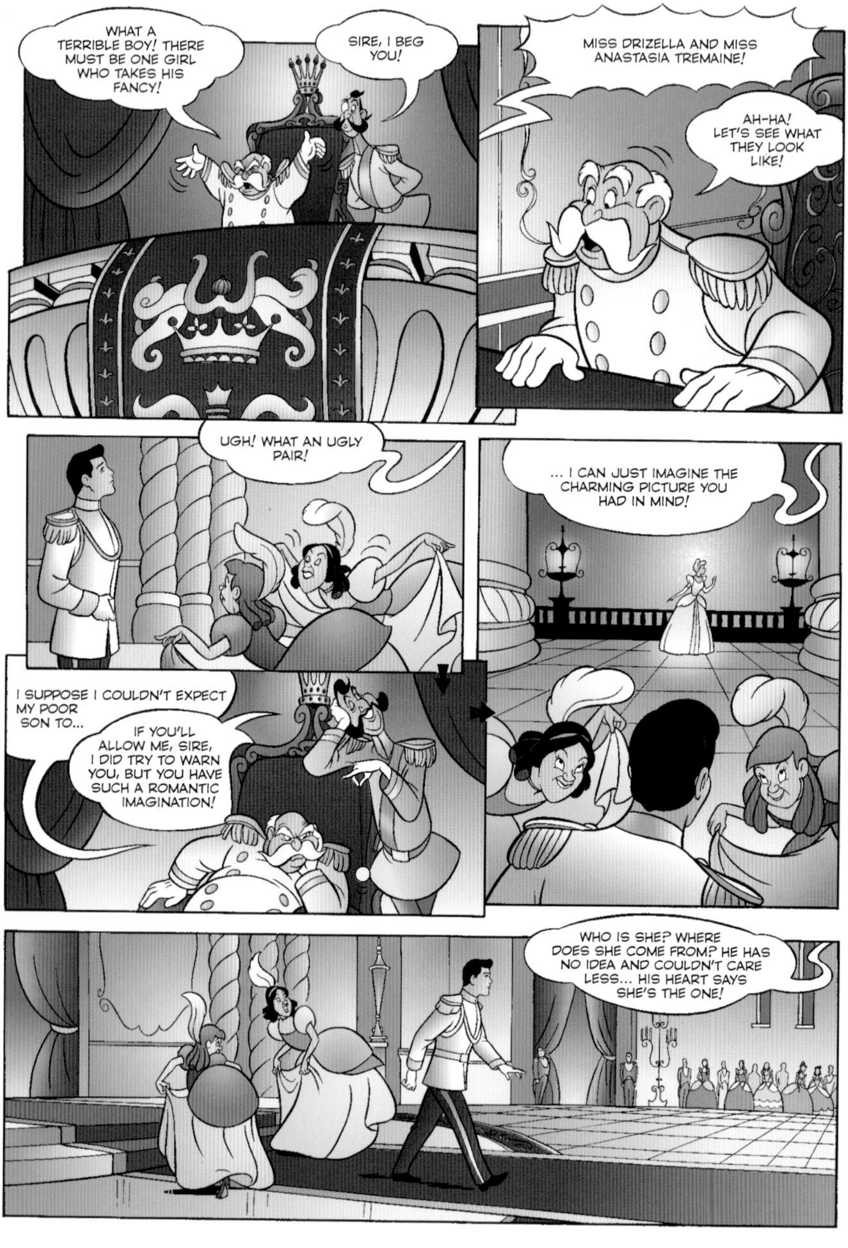
WHAT A TERRIBLE BOY! THERE MUST BE ONE GIRL WHO TAKES HIS FANCY!
SIRE, I BEG YOU!
MISS DRIZELLA AND MISS ANASTASIA TREMAINE!
AH-HA! LET'S SEE WHAT THEY LOOK LIKE!
UGH! WHAT AN UGLY PAIR!
I SUPPOSE I COULDN'T EXPECT MY POOR SON TO...
IF YOU'LL ALLOW ME, SIRE, I DID TRY TO WARN YOU, BUT YOU HAVE SUCH A ROMANTIC IMAGINATION!
... I CAN JUST IMAGINE THE CHARMING PICTURE YOU HAD IN MIND!
WHO IS SHE? WHERE DOES SHE COME FROM? HE HAS NO IDEA AND COULDN'T CARE LESS... HIS HEART SAYS SHE'S THE ONE!

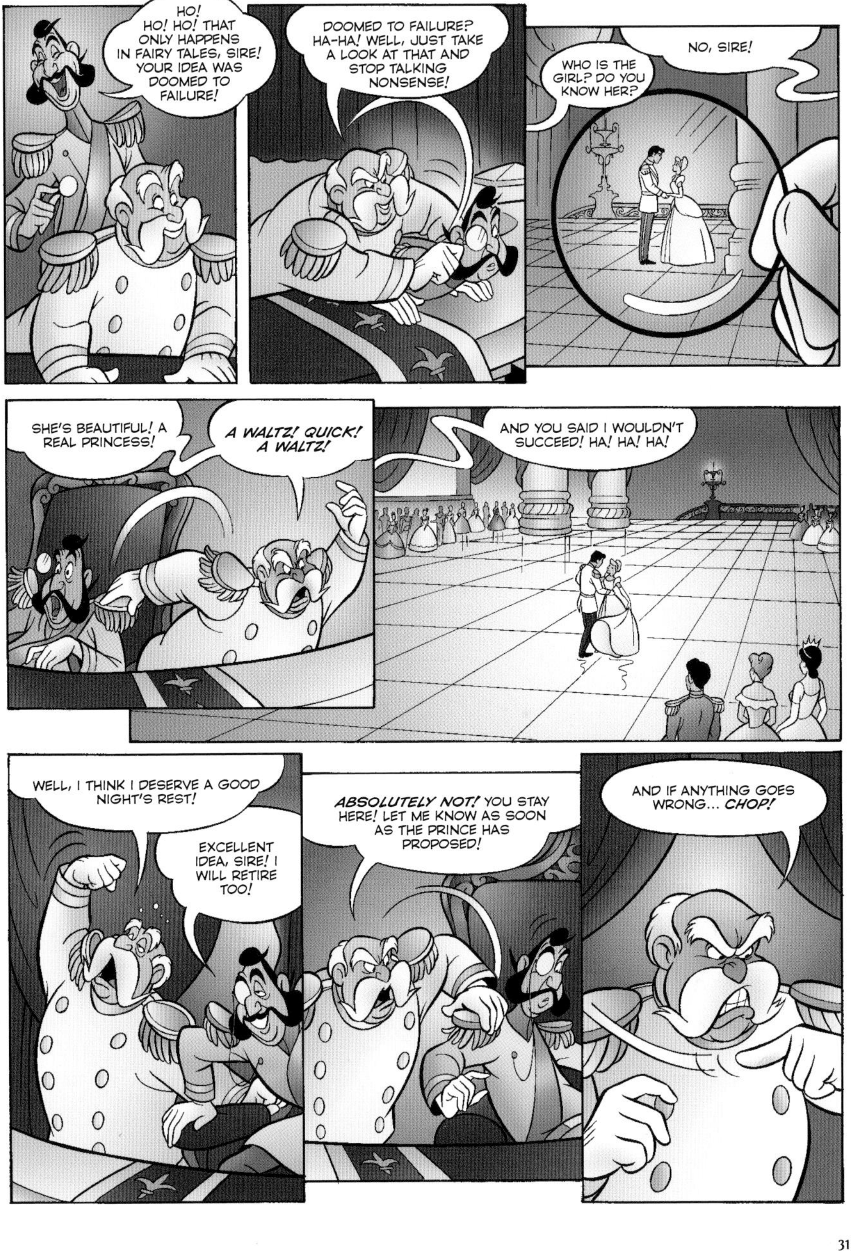
HO! HO! HO! THAT ONLY HAPPENS IN FAIRY TALES, SIRE! YOUR IDEA WAS DOOMED TO FAILURE!
DOOMED TO FAILURE? HA-HA! WELL, JUST TAKE A LOOK AT THAT AND STOP TALKING NONSENSE!
WHO IS THE GIRL? DO YOU KNOW HER?
NO, SIRE!
SHE'S BEAUTIFUL! A REAL PRINCESS!
*A WALTZ! QUICK! A WALTZ!*
AND YOU SAID I WOULDN'T SUCCEED! HA! HA! HA!
WELL, I THINK I DESERVE A GOOD NIGHT'S REST!
EXCELLENT IDEA, SIRE! I WILL RETIRE TOO!
*ABSOLUTELY NOT!* YOU STAY HERE! LET ME KNOW AS SOON AS THE PRINCE HAS PROPOSED!
AND IF ANYTHING GOES WRONG... *CHOP!*

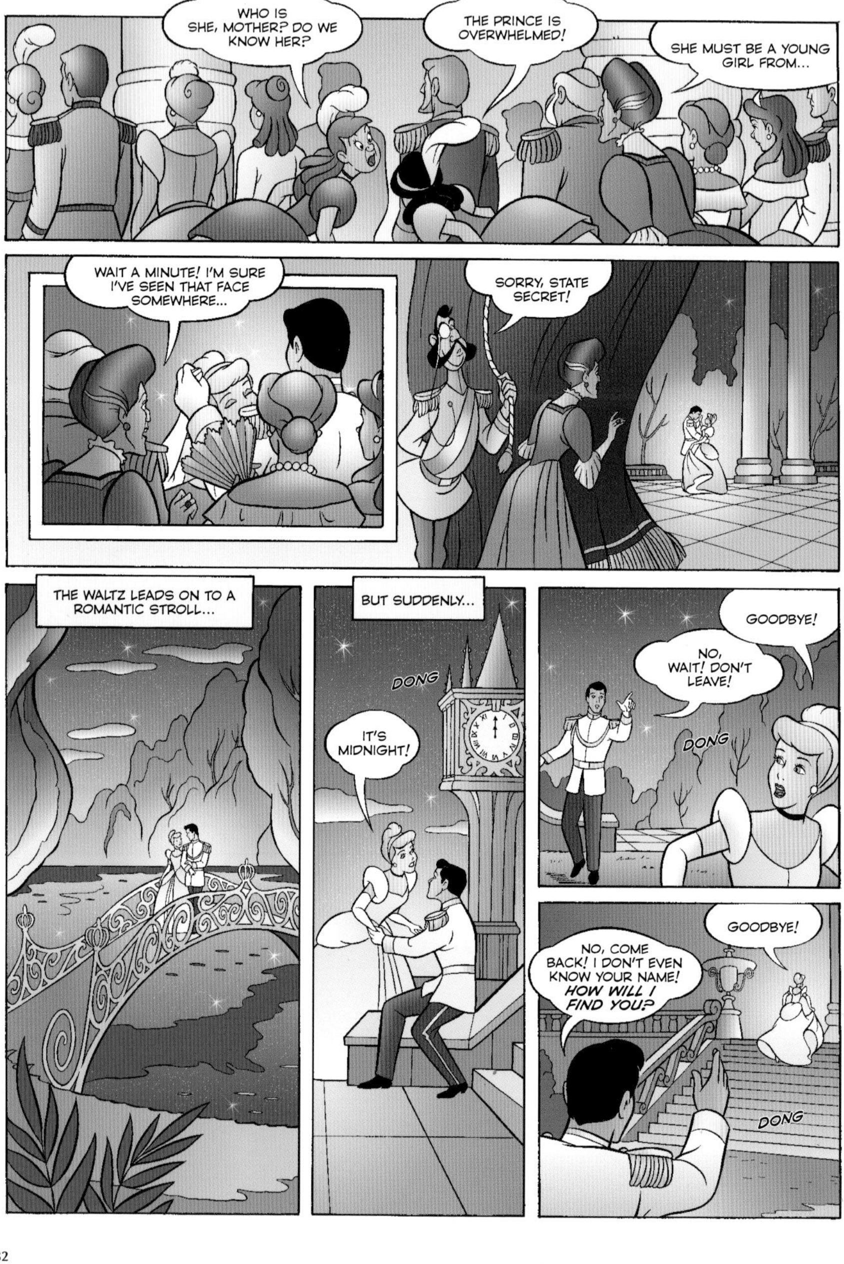
WHO IS SHE, MOTHER? DO WE KNOW HER?
THE PRINCE IS OVERWHELMED!
SHE MUST BE A YOUNG GIRL FROM...
WAIT A MINUTE! I'M SURE I'VE SEEN THAT FACE SOMEWHERE...
SORRY, STATE SECRET!
THE WALTZ LEADS ON TO A ROMANTIC STROLL...
BUT SUDDENLY...
DONG
IT'S MIDNIGHT!
GOODBYE!
NO, WAIT! DON'T LEAVE!
DONG
GOODBYE!
NO, COME BACK! I DON'T EVEN KNOW YOUR NAME! HOW WILL I FIND YOU?
DONG

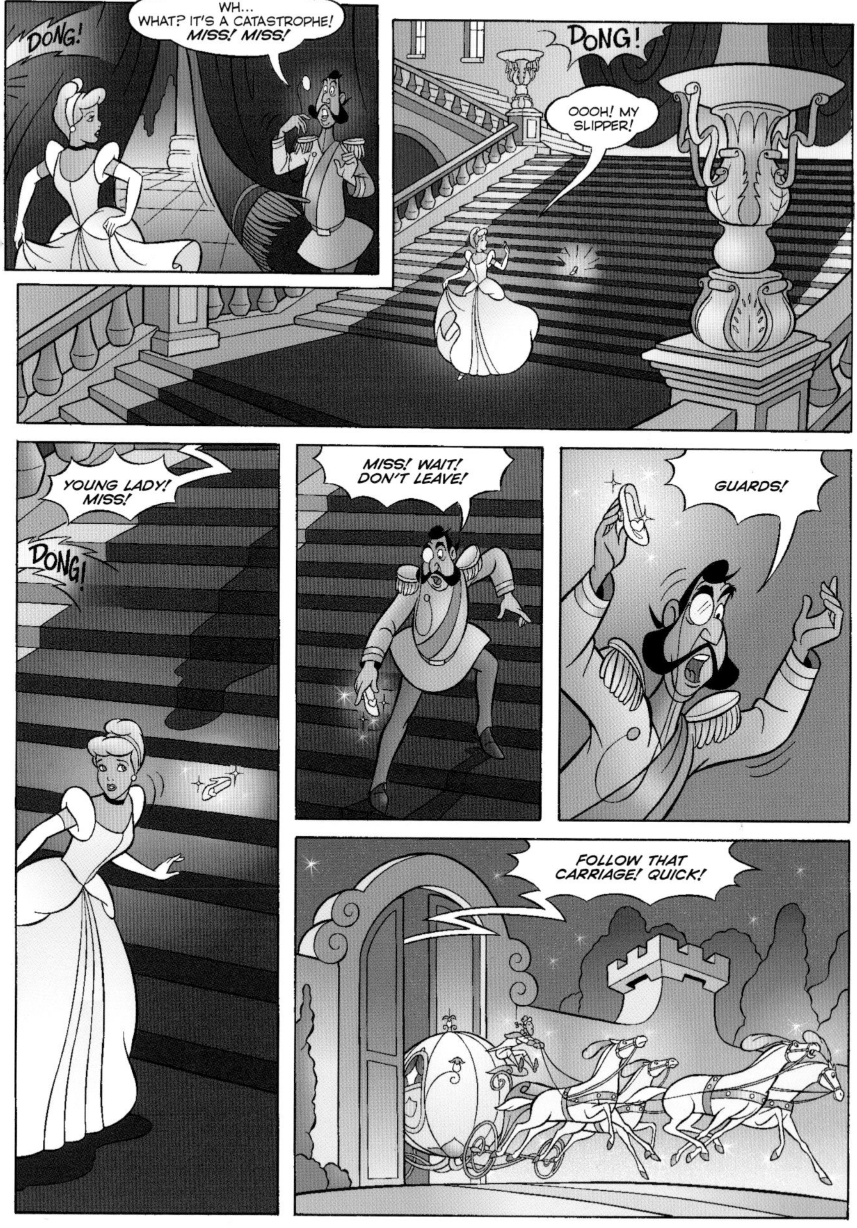
DONG!
WH...
WHAT? IT'S A CATASTROPHE!
MISS! MISS!
DONG!
OOOH! MY SLIPPER!
YOUNG LADY! MISS!
DONG!
MISS! WAIT! DON'T LEAVE!
GUARDS!
FOLLOW THAT CARRIAGE! QUICK!

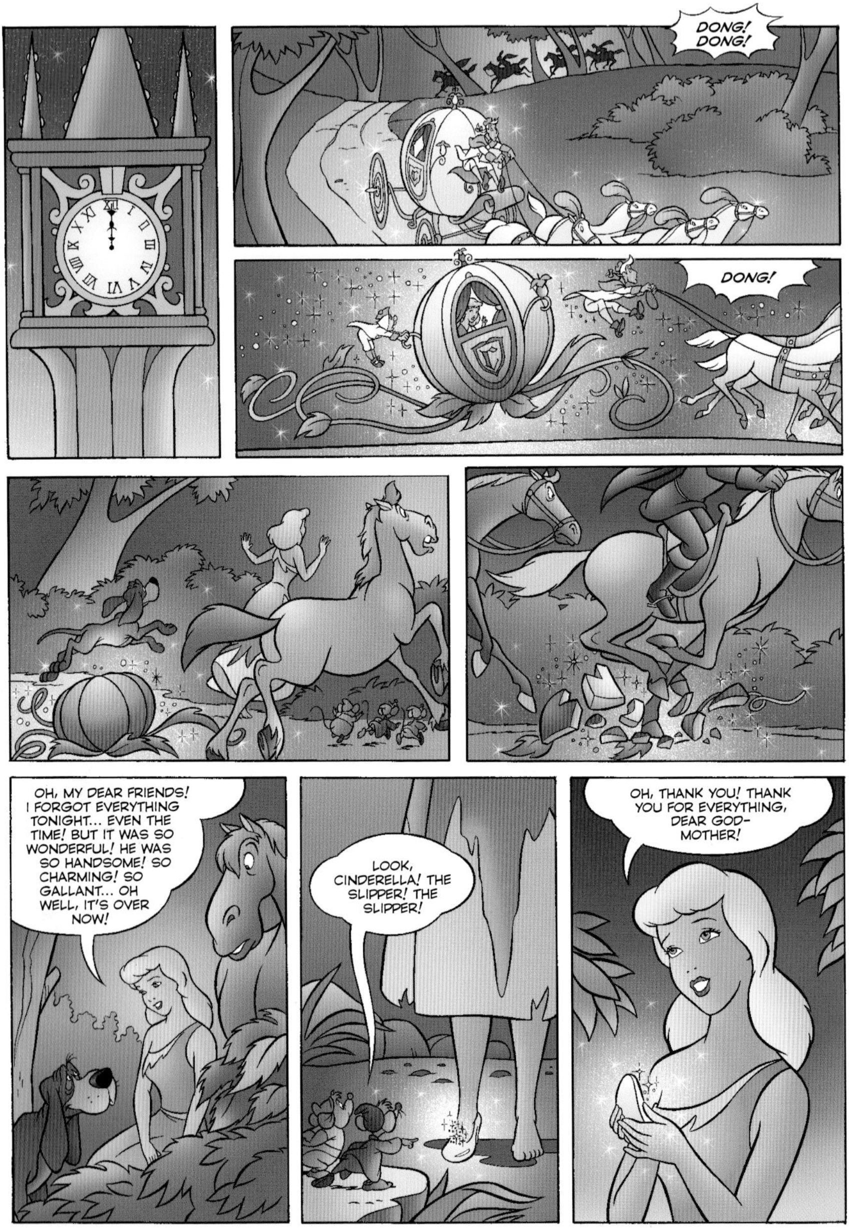
DONG! DONG!
DONG!
OH, MY DEAR FRIENDS! I FORGOT EVERYTHING TONIGHT... EVEN THE TIME! BUT IT WAS SO WONDERFUL! HE WAS SO HANDSOME! SO CHARMING! SO GALLANT... OH WELL, IT'S OVER NOW!
LOOK, CINDERELLA! THE SLIPPER! THE SLIPPER!
OH, THANK YOU! THANK YOU FOR EVERYTHING, DEAR GOD-MOTHER!

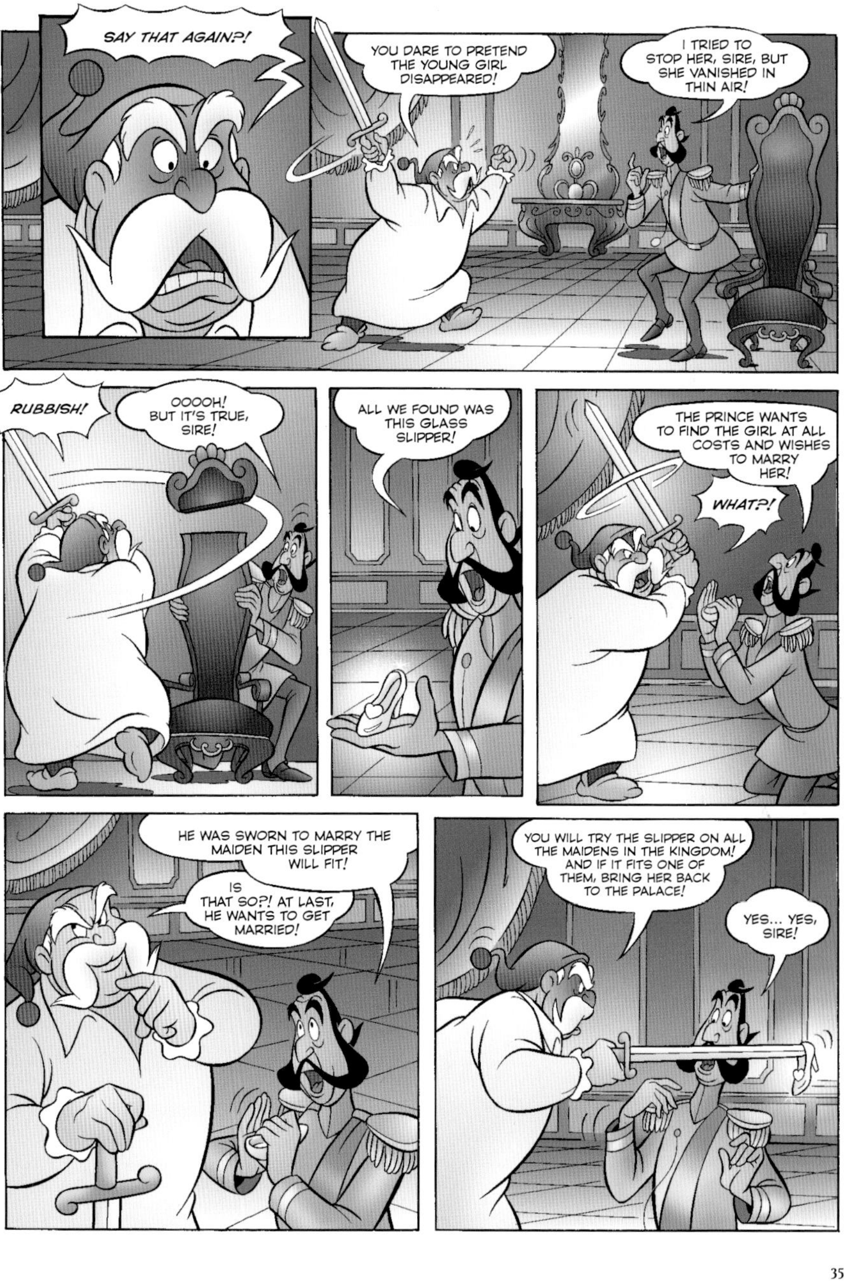
SAY THAT AGAIN?!
YOU DARE TO PRETEND THE YOUNG GIRL DISAPPEARED!
I TRIED TO STOP HER, SIRE, BUT SHE VANISHED IN THIN AIR!
RUBBISH!
OOOOH! BUT IT'S TRUE, SIRE!
ALL WE FOUND WAS THIS GLASS SLIPPER!
THE PRINCE WANTS TO FIND THE GIRL AT ALL COSTS AND WISHES TO MARRY HER!
WHAT?!
HE WAS SWORN TO MARRY THE MAIDEN THIS SLIPPER WILL FIT!
IS THAT SO?! AT LAST, HE WANTS TO GET MARRIED!
YOU WILL TRY THE SLIPPER ON ALL THE MAIDENS IN THE KINGDOM! AND IF IT FITS ONE OF THEM, BRING HER BACK TO THE PALACE!
YES... YES, SIRE!

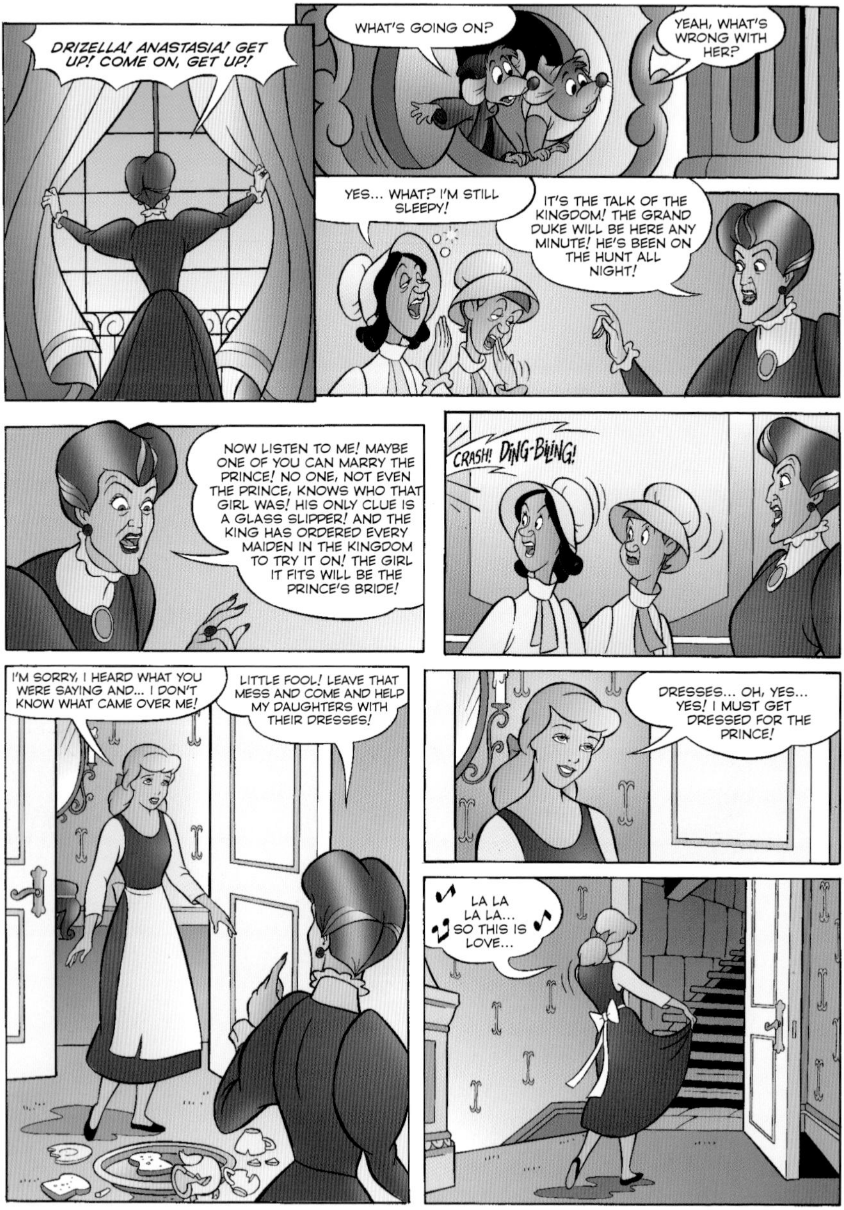

DRIZELLA! ANASTASIA! GET UP! COME ON, GET UP!
WHAT'S GOING ON?
YEAH, WHAT'S WRONG WITH HER?
YES... WHAT? I'M STILL SLEEPY!
IT'S THE TALK OF THE KINGDOM! THE GRAND DUKE WILL BE HERE ANY MINUTE! HE'S BEEN ON THE HUNT ALL NIGHT!
NOW LISTEN TO ME! MAYBE ONE OF YOU CAN MARRY THE PRINCE! NO ONE, NOT EVEN THE PRINCE, KNOWS WHO THAT GIRL WAS! HIS ONLY CLUE IS A GLASS SLIPPER! AND THE KING HAS ORDERED EVERY MAIDEN IN THE KINGDOM TO TRY IT ON! THE GIRL IT FITS WILL BE THE PRINCE'S BRIDE!
CRASH! DING-BILING!
I'M SORRY, I HEARD WHAT YOU WERE SAYING AND... I DON'T KNOW WHAT CAME OVER ME!
LITTLE FOOL! LEAVE THAT MESS AND COME AND HELP MY DAUGHTERS WITH THEIR DRESSES!
DRESSES... OH, YES... YES! I MUST GET DRESSED FOR THE PRINCE!
LA LA LA LA... SO THIS IS LOVE...

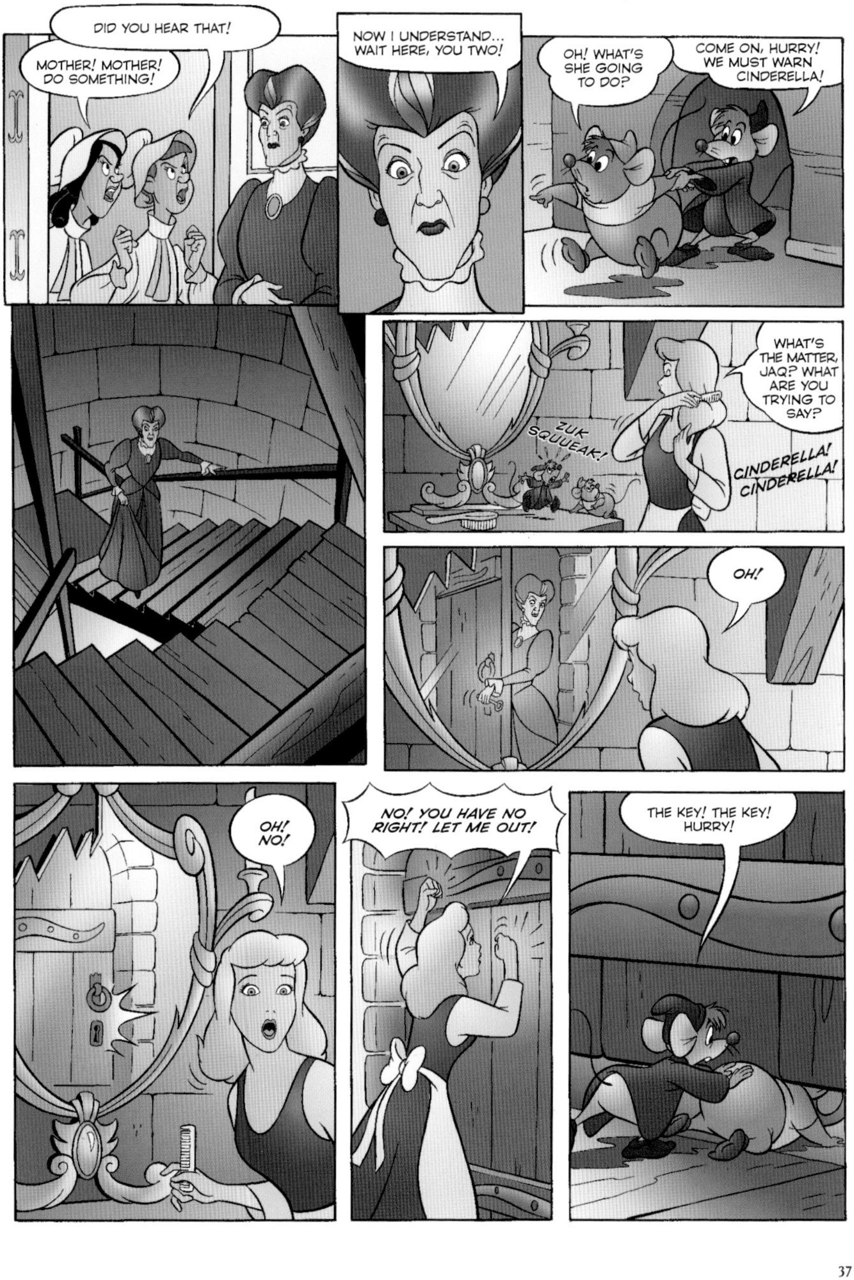
DID YOU HEAR THAT!
MOTHER! MOTHER! DO SOMETHING!
NOW I UNDERSTAND... WAIT HERE, YOU TWO!
OH! WHAT'S SHE GOING TO DO?
COME ON, HURRY! WE MUST WARN CINDERELLA!
ZUK SQUUEAK!
WHAT'S THE MATTER, JAQ? WHAT ARE YOU TRYING TO SAY?
CINDERELLA! CINDERELLA!
OH!
OH! NO!
NO! YOU HAVE NO RIGHT! LET ME OUT!
THE KEY! THE KEY! HURRY!

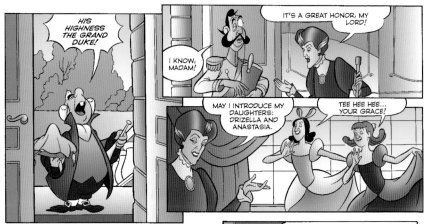

HIS HIGHNESS THE GRAND DUKE!

IT'S A GREAT HONOR, MY LORD!

I KNOW, MADAM!

MAY I INTRODUCE MY DAUGHTERS: DRIZELLA AND ANASTASIA.

TEE HEE HEE... YOUR GRACE!

HIS GRACE WILL READ THE ROYAL PROCLAMATION!

ALL HIS MAJESTY'S LOYAL SUBJECTS ARE INFORMED THAT AN INQUIRY ON A GLASS SLIPPER HAS BEEN ORDERED THIS VERY DAY...

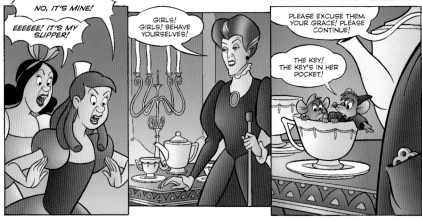

NO, IT'S MINE!

EEEEEE! IT'S MY SLIPPER!

GIRLS! GIRLS! BEHAVE YOURSELVES!

PLEASE EXCUSE THEM, YOUR GRACE! PLEASE CONTINUE!

THE KEY! THE KEY'S IN HER POCKET!

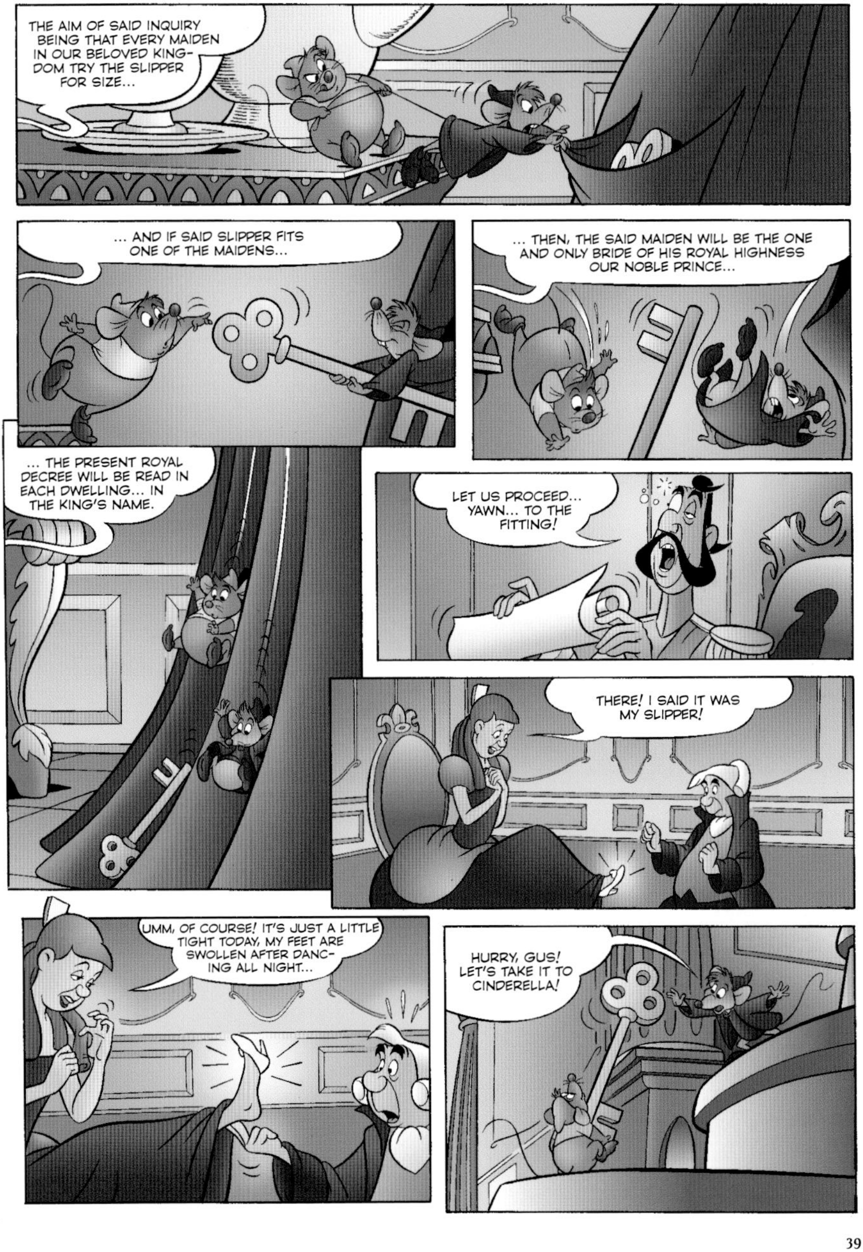
THE AIM OF SAID INQUIRY BEING THAT EVERY MAIDEN IN OUR BELOVED KINGDOM TRY THE SLIPPER FOR SIZE...
... AND IF SAID SLIPPER FITS ONE OF THE MAIDENS...
... THEN, THE SAID MAIDEN WILL BE THE ONE AND ONLY BRIDE OF HIS ROYAL HIGHNESS OUR NOBLE PRINCE...
... THE PRESENT ROYAL DECREE WILL BE READ IN EACH DWELLING... IN THE KING'S NAME.
LET US PROCEED... YAWN... TO THE FITTING!
THERE! I SAID IT WAS MY SLIPPER!
UMM, OF COURSE! IT'S JUST A LITTLE TIGHT TODAY, MY FEET ARE SWOLLEN AFTER DANCING ALL NIGHT...
HURRY, GUS! LET'S TAKE IT TO CINDERELLA!

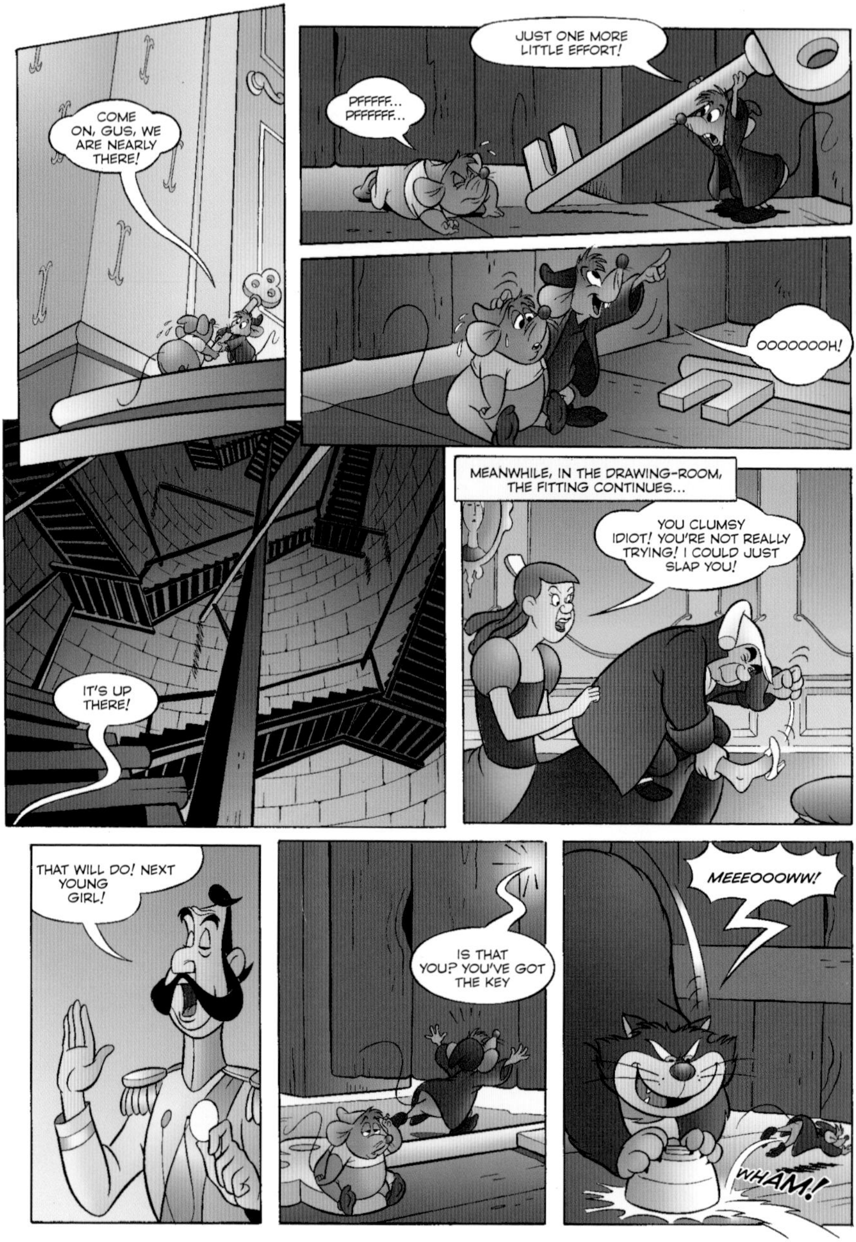
COME ON, GUS, WE ARE NEARLY THERE!
PFFFFF... PFFFFFF...
JUST ONE MORE LITTLE EFFORT!
OOOOOOOH!
IT'S UP THERE!
MEANWHILE, IN THE DRAWING-ROOM, THE FITTING CONTINUES...
YOU CLUMSY IDIOT! YOU'RE NOT REALLY TRYING! I COULD JUST SLAP YOU!
THAT WILL DO! NEXT YOUNG GIRL!
IS THAT YOU? YOU'VE GOT THE KEY
MEEEOOOWW!
WHAM!

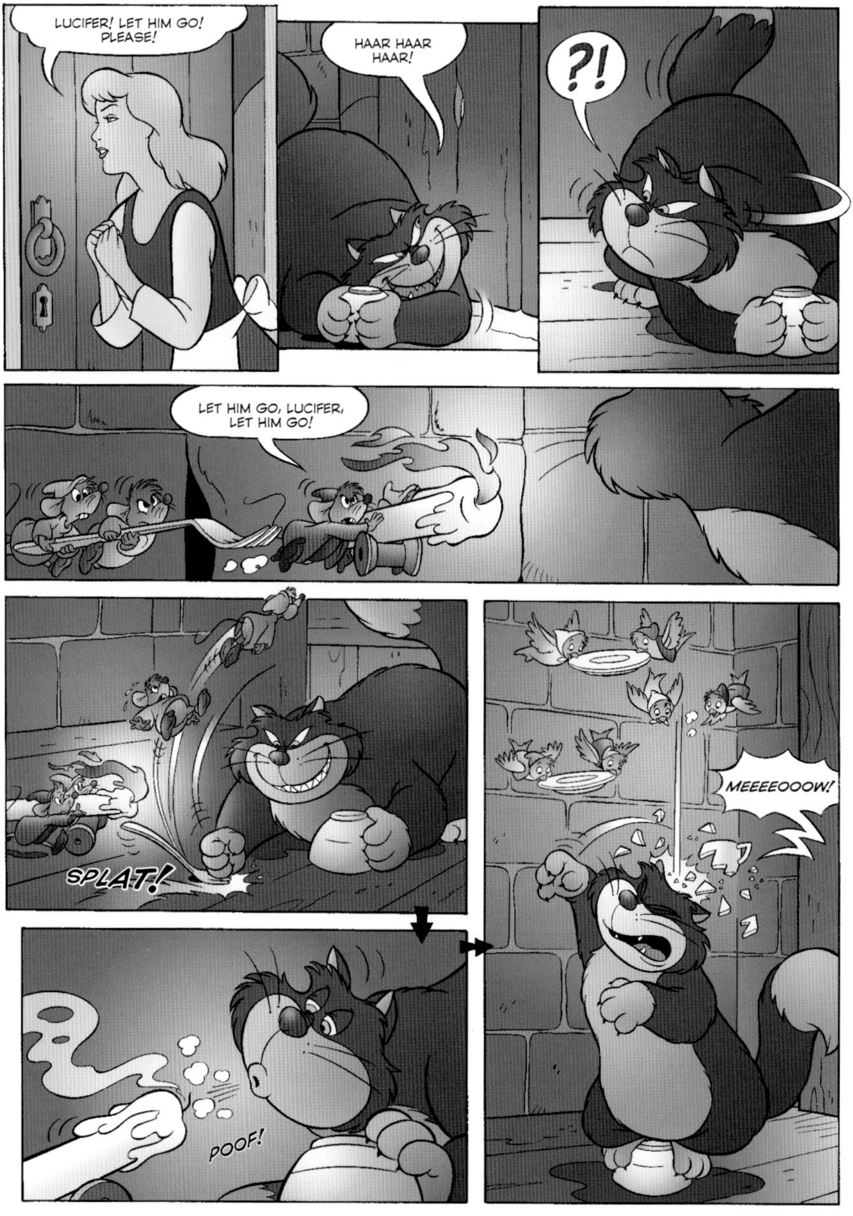
LUCIFER! LET HIM GO! PLEASE!
HAAR HAAR HAAR!
?!
LET HIM GO, LUCIFER, LET HIM GO!
SPLAT!
POOF!
MEEEEOOOW!

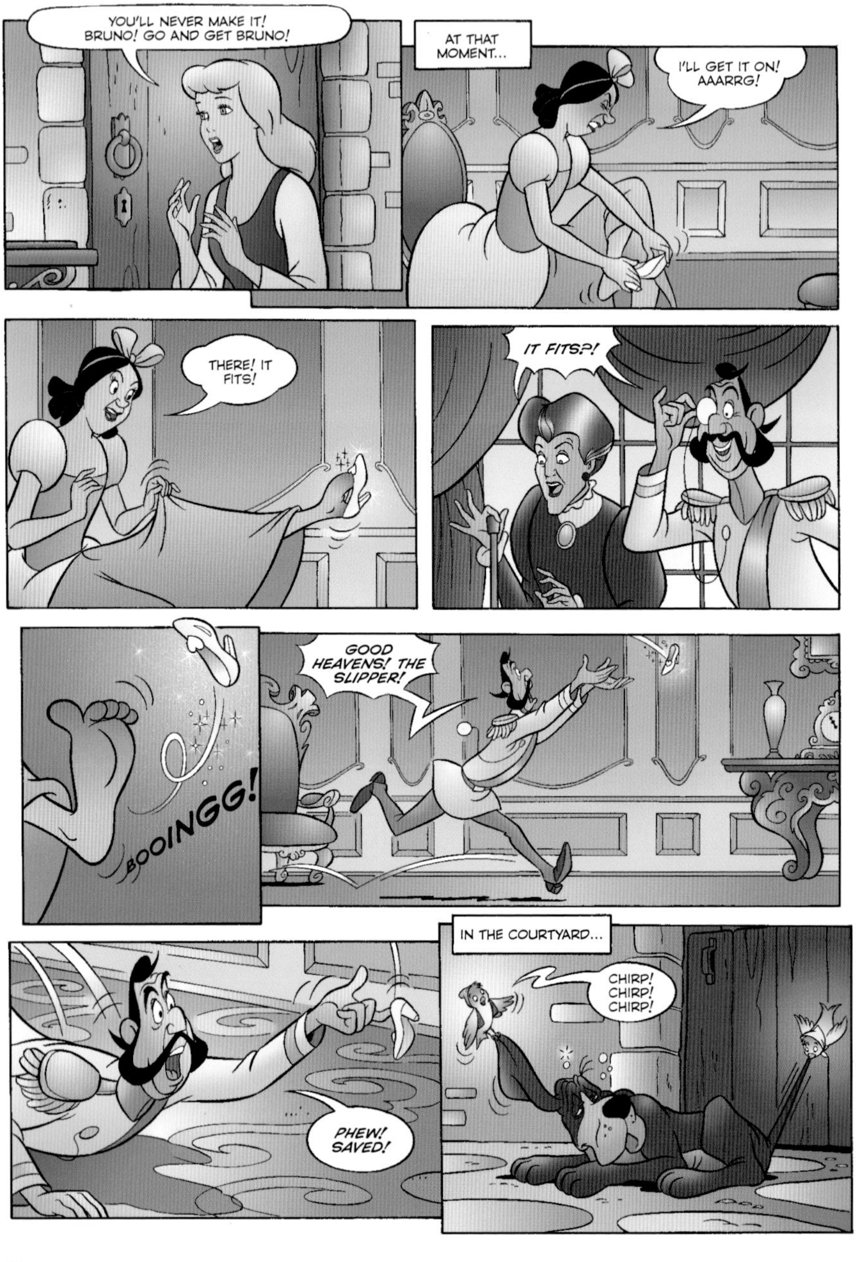

YOU'LL NEVER MAKE IT! BRUNO! GO AND GET BRUNO!
AT THAT MOMENT...
I'LL GET IT ON! AAARRG!
THERE! IT FITS!
IT FITS?!
BOOINGG!
GOOD HEAVENS! THE SLIPPER!
PHEW! SAVED!
IN THE COURTYARD...
CHIRP! CHIRP! CHIRP!

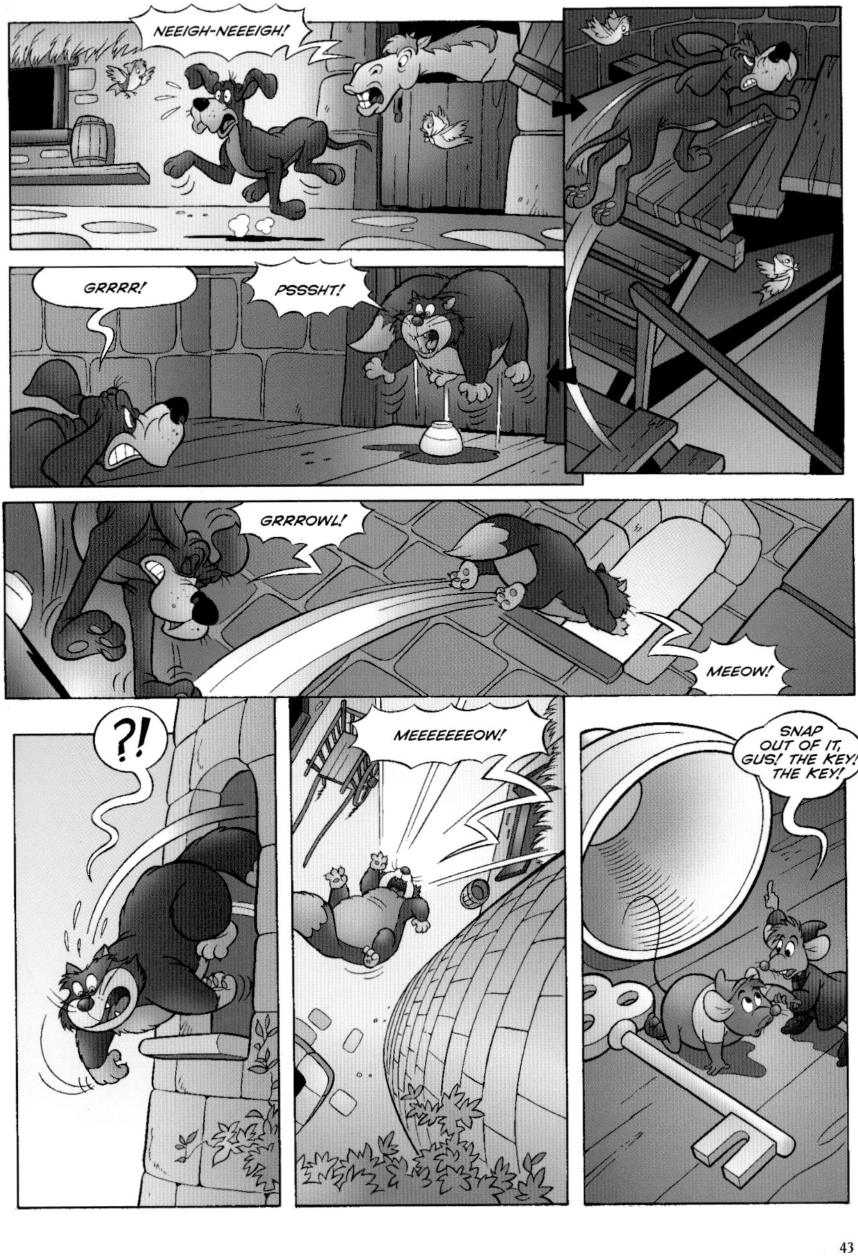
NEEIGH-NEEEIGH!
GRRRR!
PSSSHT!
GRRROWL!
MEEOW!
?!
MEEEEEEEOW!
SNAP OUT OF IT, GUS! THE KEY! THE KEY!

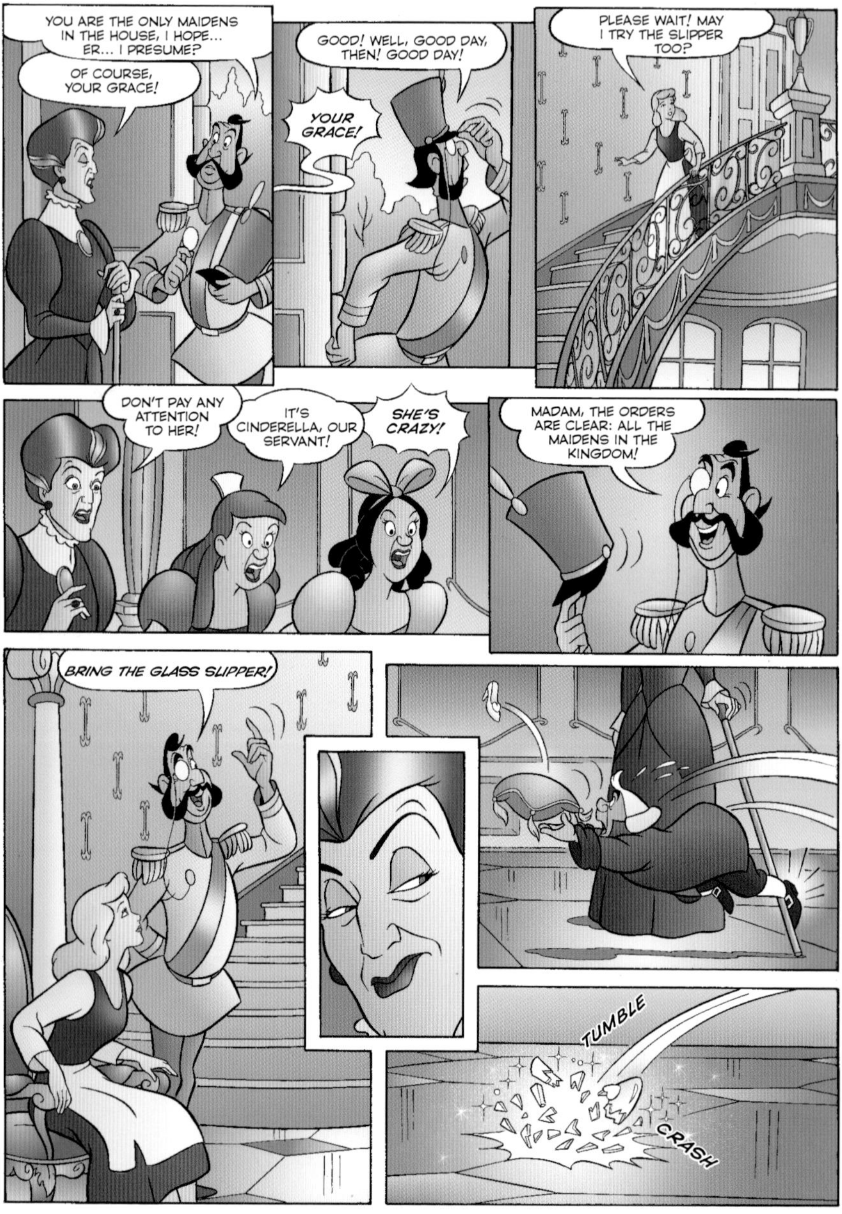
YOU ARE THE ONLY MAIDENS IN THE HOUSE, I HOPE... ER... I PRESUME?
OF COURSE, YOUR GRACE!
GOOD! WELL, GOOD DAY, THEN! GOOD DAY!
YOUR GRACE!
PLEASE WAIT! MAY I TRY THE SLIPPER TOO?
DON'T PAY ANY ATTENTION TO HER!
IT'S CINDERELLA, OUR SERVANT!
SHE'S CRAZY!
MADAM, THE ORDERS ARE CLEAR: ALL THE MAIDENS IN THE KINGDOM!
BRING THE GLASS SLIPPER!
TUMBLE
CRASH

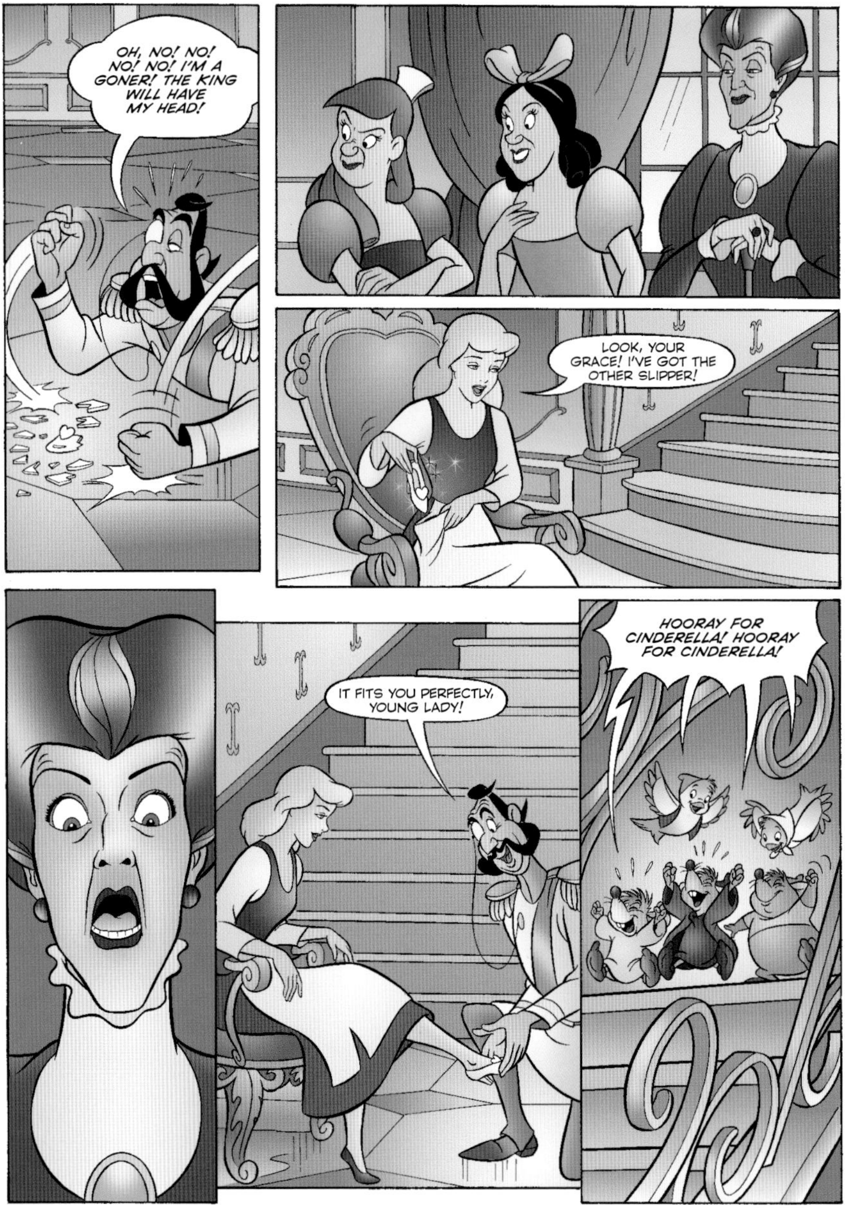
OH, NO! NO! NO! NO! I'M A GONER! THE KING WILL HAVE MY HEAD!
LOOK, YOUR GRACE! I'VE GOT THE OTHER SLIPPER!
IT FITS YOU PERFECTLY, YOUNG LADY!
HOORAY FOR CINDERELLA! HOORAY FOR CINDERELLA!

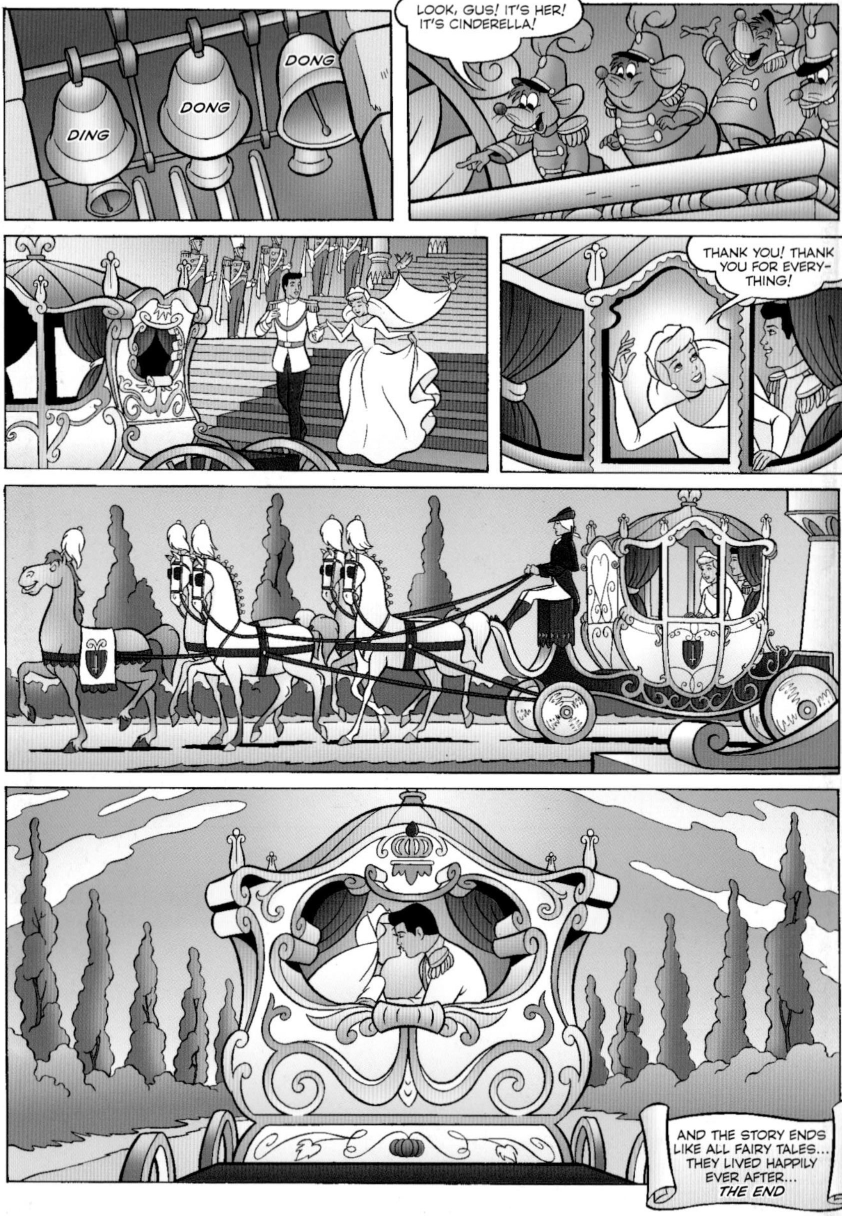
DING
DONG
DONG
LOOK, GUS! IT'S HER! IT'S CINDERELLA!
THANK YOU! THANK YOU FOR EVERYTHING!
AND THE STORY ENDS LIKE ALL FAIRY TALES... THEY LIVED HAPPILY EVER AFTER...
THE END

SCRIPT ADAPTATION
**Regis Maine**

PENCILS
**Mario Cortes**

INKS
**Comicup Studios**

LETTERS
**Erika Terriquez**

## DARK HORSE BOOKS

PRESIDENT AND PUBLISHER **Mike Richardson**
COLLECTION EDITOR **Freddye Miller** COLLECTION ASSISTANT EDITOR **Judy Khuu**
DESIGNER **Sarah Terry** DIGITAL ART TECHNICIAN **Samantha Hummer**

Neil Hankerson Executive Vice President • Tom Weddle Chief Financial Officer • Randy Stradley Vice President of Publishing • Nick McWhorter Chief Business Development Officer • Dale LaFountain Chief Information Officer • Matt Parkinson Vice President of Marketing • Cara Niece Vice President of Production and Scheduling • Mark Bernardi Vice President of Book Trade and Digital Sales • Ken Lizzi General Counsel • Dave Marshall Editor in Chief • Davey Estrada Editorial Director • Chris Warner Senior Books Editor • Cary Grazzini Director of Specialty Projects • Lia Ribacchi Art Director • Vanessa Todd-Holmes Director of Print Purchasing • Matt Dryer Director of Digital Art and Prepress • Michael Gombos Senior Director of Licensed Publications • Kari Yadro Director of Custom Programs • Kari Torson Director of International Licensing • Sean Brice Director of Trade Sales

DISNEY PUBLISHING WORLDWIDE GLOBAL MAGAZINES, COMICS AND PARTWORKS

PUBLISHER Lynn Waggoner • EDITORIAL TEAM Bianca Coletti (Director, Magazines), Guido Frazzini (Director, Comics), Carlotta Quattrocolo (Executive Editor), Stefano Ambrosio (Executive Editor, New IP), Camilla Vedove (Senior Manager, Editorial Development), Behnoosh Khalili (Senior Editor), Julie Dorris (Senior Editor), Mina Riazi (Assistant Editor), Gabriela Capasso (Assistant Editor) • DESIGN Enrico Soave (Senior Designer) • ART Ken Shue (VP, Global Art), Manny Mederos (Senior Illustration Manager, Comics and Magazines), Roberto Santillo (Creative Director), Marco Ghiglione (Creative Manager), Stefano Attardi (Illustration Manager) • PORTFOLIO MANAGEMENT Olivia Ciancarelli (Director) • BUSINESS & MARKETING Mariantonietta Galla (Senior Manager, Franchise), Virpi Korhonen (Editorial Manager)

Published by Dark Horse Books
A division of Dark Horse Comics LLC
10956 SE Main Street | Milwaukie, OR 97222

DarkHorse.com

To find a comics shop in your area, visit comicshoplocator.com

First Dark Horse Books edition: February 2020
ISBN 978-1-50671-737-1
Digital ISBN 978-1-50671-746-3

1 3 5 7 9 10 8 6 4 2
Printed in China

The classic tale of
## Snow White and the Seven Dwarfs
reawakens!

Relive the beloved Disney fairy tale through the
first-person perspective of Snow White herself!

978-1-50671-462-2 • $12.99